What if he couldn't keep her safe on his ranch?

His hand lingered against her cheek, his touch warm and firm, full of strength tempered by gentle concern.

"It felt real," she said, tears stinging her eyes. She'd felt the man's anger. His hate.

"Nobody's out there," Riley assured her, pushing her wet hair out of her face.

Her breath hitched, catching somewhere in the middle of her chest.

She gazed up into his shadowed eyes, where something glittered, fierce and white-hot, stealing the air from her lungs. His fingers tangled in the hair at her temples, trapping her.

He was going to kiss her. And she was going to let him. Right now she needed comfort, she needed something good to wipe out what she'd been through, if only for a short time.

As she rose to meet him, his mouth descended, hard and hungry against hers.

She needed Riley.

PAULA GRAVES

CASE FILE: CANYON CREEK, WYOMING

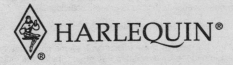

TORONTO • NEW YORK • LONDON
AMSTERDAM • PARIS • SYDNEY • HAMBURG
STOCKHOLM • ATHENS • TOKYO • MILAN • MADRID
PRAGUE • WARSAW • BUDAPEST • AUCKLAND

For my brother Dennis, who taught me how to fish, and whose wild imagination always sparked my own.

Recycling programs
for this product may
not exist in your area.

ISBN-13: 978-0-373-69450-1

CASE FILE: CANYON CREEK, WYOMING

ABOUT THE AUTHOR

Alabama native Paula Graves wrote her first book, a mystery starring herself and her neighborhood friends, at the age of six. A voracious reader, Paula loves books that pair tantalizing mystery with compelling romance. When she's not reading or writing, she works as a creative director for a Birmingham advertising agency and spends time with her family and friends. She is a member of Southern Magic Romance Writers, Heart of Dixie Romance Writers and Romance Writers of America.

Paula invites readers to visit her Web site, www.paulagraves.com.

Books by Paula Graves

HARLEQUIN INTRIGUE

*Cooper Justice

CAST OF CHARACTERS

Hannah Cooper—After barely escaping a roadside attack, the fishing camp guide puts her vacation on hold and her life on the line to help a driven Wyoming lawman catch an elusive killer. But will she risk her heart on the widowed cowboy, as well?

Riley Patterson—Since his wife, Emily, was murdered three years earlier, the Wyoming cop has been obsessed with finding her killer. Hannah could be the key to solving the case—and breaking down his barriers.

Jack Drummond—Riley's brother-in-law is back in town for the first time since his sister's funeral. Will his new friendship with Hannah get in the way of Riley's investigation?

Jim Tanner—The Teton County sheriff wants Hannah to be the bait in a trap to catch the killer. Is he putting her in danger without calculating the risks?

Joe Garrison—Riley's boss and best friend understands Riley's driving need for justice. He needs to keep his friend from crossing the line in his hunt for the killer.

Ken Lassiter—Hannah's fishing client seems like an ordinary guy. But should she trust anyone while a killer is on the loose?

Aaron Cooper—When a Wyoming cop shows up in Alabama, warning him that his little sister is in trouble, the deputy sheriff springs into action.

Chapter One

The flashing blue light in the rearview mirror came out of nowhere, cutting through the cool shadows of the waning afternoon. Hannah Cooper glanced at the rental car's speedometer needle, which hovered just under sixty. The speed limit was sixty-five on this stretch of Wyoming's Highway 287, so she wasn't speeding.

Maybe he just wanted her to move aside to make it easier to pass her on the two-lane highway. She edged the Pontiac toward the narrow shoulder, but the car behind her slowed as well, making no attempt to go around her. The driver waved out the window for her to pull all the way over.

Damn it. She released a slow breath and looked for somewhere to pull to the side. The highway shoulder barely existed on this stretch of winding road, the grassy edge rising quickly to meet the dense stand of pines lining the highway. Hannah spotted a widening of the shoulder a few yards ahead. She slowed and pulled over, cutting the engine.

Tamping down a nervous flutter in her belly, she lowered the window with one hand while pulling her wallet from her purse with the other. Outside the window, footsteps approached. She turned to face the lawman. "Is something wrong?"

She got a brief glimpse of weathered jeans and a shiny silver belt buckle before the man's hand—snugly tucked into latex gloves—whipped up into the window and sprayed something wet and stinging in her face.

Her gasp of surprise drew a spray of fiery heat into her mouth and throat, and her eyes slammed closed, acid tears seeping from between her lids. *Pepper spray,* she realized, gagging as fire filled her lungs with every wheezing breath. Coughing, she tried to reorient herself in a world turned upside down.

She felt a rough hand on the back of her neck, pushing her forward toward the steering wheel with a sharp thrust. She threw herself sideways, avoiding all but a glancing blow of her cheekbone against the steering wheel. The shock of pain faded quickly compared to the lingering agony of the pepper spray. Panic rose as she felt the man's hand groping for her again.

Don't ever let them get you out of the car.

The warning that filled her foggy mind spoke in her brother Aaron's voice. Aaron, the cop, who never let pass any opportunity to give her advice about personal safety.

If they get you out of your car, you're dead.

The man's hand tangled briefly in her hair then retreated. A soft snapping sound outside the car made her jerk her head toward the open window, and she forced her eyelids open, blinking hard to clear her blurry vision. Through a film of white-hot pain, she saw her assailant's right hand sliding something black and metallic from a side holster.

Gun.

It snagged coming out of the holster, giving her the distraction she needed. Spotting his left hand resting on the car-door frame for balance, she rammed her elbow on to the back of his hand, crushing his fingers against the door. Something hard and metallic cracked against her elbow bone—a ring? It sent pain jarring up her arm, but she ignored it as he spat out a loud curse and pulled his hand free, just as she'd hoped.

She turned the key in the ignition. The rented Pontiac G6 roared to life and she jerked it into Drive, ramming the accelerator pedal to the floor.

The Pontiac shimmied across the sandy ground, the right back wheel teetering precariously along the edge of the dipping shoulder, but she muscled it back on to the highway and pointed its nose toward the long stretch of road ahead.

She groped on the seat next to her for the bottle of water she'd picked up from a vending machine at a gas station a few miles back. Grappling with the cap, she opened the bottle and splashed water in her eyes, trying to wash out enough of the burning spray to help her see as she drove. It helped the stinging pain in her eyes but did nothing to stop the burning on her skin and in her nose and throat.

Think, Hannah. Think.

She felt for her purse, which held her cell phone, but it must have fallen to the floorboard. She couldn't risk trying to find it. Though she could barely see, barely breathe, she didn't dare slow down, taking the curves at scary speeds. There had to be civilization somewhere ahead, she promised herself, shivering with shock and pain. Just another mile or so….

She peered blindly at the rearview mirror, trying to see if the car with the blue light was following. She'd rounded a curve that put a hilly stand of pines between her car and the waning daylight backlighting the Wyoming Rockies. Behind her, night had already begun to fall in murky purple shadows, hiding any sign of her assailant from view. Maybe she'd bought herself enough time.

She just had to keep going. Surely somewhere ahead she'd run into people who could help her.

She wiped her watering eyes, trying to see through the gloom. More than once over the next endless, excruciating mile, she nearly drove off the road, but soon the highway curved again, and the mountains came back into view, rising with violent beauty into the copper-penny sky. And just a mile or so ahead, gleaming like a beacon to her burning eyes, a truck stop sprawled along the side of the highway.

She headed her car toward the lighted sign, daring only a quick glance in her rearview mirror. She spotted a car behind her, a black dot in the lowering darkness. It seemed to be coming fast, growing larger and more threatening as the distance between her and the truck stop diminished.

Heart pounding, Hannah rammed the accelerator to the floor again, pushing the Pontiac to its limits. It shuddered beneath her, the engine whining, but the distance to the truck stop was yards now, close enough that she could make out men milling in the parking lot.

Behind her, the pursuing car fell back, as if he realized the foolishness of trying to overtake her so close to a truck stop full of witnesses. Shaking with relief, she aimed her car at the blurry span of the truck-stop driveway.

The sun dipped behind the mountains just as she made the turn, casting a sudden shadow across the entrance. The unexpected gloom, combined with her blurred vision, hid a dangerous obstacle until it was too late. Her right front wheel hit the rocky outcropping that edged the driveway and sent the car lurching out of control.

Fighting the wheel, she managed to avoid a large gas-tanker truck parked at the far edge of the truck-stop parking lot, but a scrubby pine loomed out of the darkness right in her path. She slammed on her brakes, but it was too late.

She hit the tree head on, and the world went black.

IN CANYON CREEK, WYOMING, night had long since fallen in cool, blue shadows tinted faint purple by the last whisper of sunset rimming the ridges to the west. With sunset had come the glow of streetlamps lining Main Street, painting the sidewalks below with circles of gold.

From his office window on the second floor of the Canyon Creek Police Department, Deputy Chief Riley Patterson had a bird's-eye view of the town he protected, though few people remained in town at this time of night. Most of the stores had shut down a couple of hours earlier, though a light still glowed in the hardware store across the street. After a moment, even that light extinguished, and Riley spotted storekeeper Dave Logan locking the store's front door, his dog Rufus waiting patiently by his side.

Riley turned from the window and sank into his desk chair, his gaze lifting to the large, round clock on the wall. At seven-forty on a Tuesday evening, Riley was one of four people left in the building, but up here on the second floor, he might as well be the only person. The quiet was like a living thing this time of night, unbroken for the most part, though a few minutes earlier he'd heard the fax go off in the chief's office. He'd check it before he left for home.

He worked late most evenings, in part because he liked the quiet time to catch up on the paperwork that took up most of his time these days, but mostly because the alternative was going home to his empty house.

He worked his way through a handful of reports the day-shift officers had left on his desk, making notes on interviews that needed follow-ups and putting them in the outbox for his secretary to file in the morning. Then he leaned back in his chair and stared at the ceiling, willing himself to grab his jacket and keys and head home before he started worrying himself the way he knew he'd begun to worry his friends and colleagues.

His desk phone rang before he could move, shattering the quiet. He dropped his feet to the floor and checked the number on the caller ID display. It was Joe Garrison, his boss and lifelong friend. Riley grabbed the receiver. "I'm about to head home, I swear—"

"Just got a call from the Teton County Sheriff," Joe interrupted briskly. "Attempted abduction on Highway 287 late this afternoon. Female victim, mid-twenties."

Riley felt a twinge of unease. "Deceased?"

"No, but I don't know any more details yet. It's Teton County's jurisdiction, but the sheriff gave me a courtesy call. His department should be faxing the details over any minute."

"The fax rang a minute ago. I'll check." Riley put Joe on hold and walked into the chief's office. He grabbed the handful of sheets from the fax tray and scanned them on the way back to his office. Standard BOLO—Be On Lookout— notice, short on details. The victim apparently hadn't gotten a good look at her attacker.

Riley reached his desk and picked up the phone. "Still there?"

"For the moment, although Jane's giving me come-hither looks that are getting a little hard to resist," Joe answered, laughter tinting his voice. "Anything on the BOLO we need to worry about?"

"According to the victim, the assailant was driving a police car, although she doesn't seem sure whether it was a marked car or not. The guy had a blue light on the roof, but it might have been a detachable one." Riley scanned further. "Not much in the way of a description, either, beyond what he was wearing."

"Odd," Joe said.

The next words Riley read made his blood go cold. A faint buzzing noise filled his ears as he read the information again.

"Riley?" Joe prodded on the other end of the line.

Riley cleared his throat, but when he spoke, his voice still came out raspy and tight. "She was pepper-sprayed. In the face."

There was a brief silence on the other end of the line while the implications sank in for Joe. A second later, he said, "I'll be there in ten minutes." He hung up without saying goodbye.

Riley put down the phone and stared at the BOLO, rereading the passage one more time to make sure he hadn't misread. But the words remained unchanged—oleoresin capsicum found on the victim's face, clothing and in her mucus and saliva.

He sank heavily into his desk chair, his hand automatically reaching for the bottom drawer to his right. He pulled it open and took out a dog-eared manila folder, the only thing that occupied the drawer. He thumbed through the familiar pages inside the file folder, searching for the three-year-old Natrona County coroner's report. His breath caught when he read the decedent's name—Patterson, Emily D.—but he dragged his gaze away from the name to the toxicology report on the pages stapled behind the death certificate.

Oleoresin capsicum. It had been found in her eyes, nose, throat and lungs, preserved, ironically, by the plastic sheeting her killer had wrapped her in before sinking her body in a lake off Highway 20.

He heard footsteps pounding up the stairs outside his office. Joe burst through the doorway, his wife, Jane, right behind him. Joe grabbed the fax pages from Riley's desk while Jane crossed to put her hand on Riley's shoulder, her green eyes warm with compassion. "You okay?" she asked.

He nodded, putting the coroner's report back into the file folder and sliding it into the open drawer.

"This is six," Joe said, settling on to the edge of Riley's desk with the fax pages in his hands.

"Six that we know of," Riley added grimly. "And we're not sure about a couple of them." The plastic sheet wrapped around the bodies of two of the victims hadn't protected them from the water where their bodies had been dumped.

"The plastic sheeting was enough of an MO for me," Joe said firmly. "If this one hadn't gotten away, she'd have shown up in a lake or river somewhere around here, wrapped in plastic, too. Maybe this time, the FBI will finally see the pattern."

The FBI didn't want to see the pattern, Riley knew. He'd tried to get the feds involved the minute he'd started piecing together the murders three years ago, when Emily had become one of the killer's victims. They hadn't been interested. "The connection was too nebulous" or some such B.S.

"I'll give Jim Tanner a call in the morning," Joe said, referring to the Teton County Sheriff. "He owes me a favor."

Jane put her hand on Riley's shoulder again. "Come home with us for dinner," she said. "It's nothing much—just some leftover barbecue, but we have plenty of it."

"Even with her eating for three," Joe added with a smile.

"Two," Jane corrected with a roll of her green eyes, "although one of us is half cowboy, so you may have a point."

Riley tried to smile at the banter, but it stung a little, even though he was happy as hell that his old friend had finally found a little happiness in his roller-coaster of a life. Seeing Joe and Jane so clearly happy, so clearly in love, was a reminder of all he'd lost three years ago when Emily had died.

"Actually, I think I'm just going to head home and try to get some sleep so I'll be fresh in the morning," he lied, even as a plan began to form in his restless mind. He gave Jane a quick kiss on the cheek and nodded toward the door. "Let's get out of here and I'll talk to you both tomorrow."

He could see a hint of suspicion in Joe's expression as the three of them walked out to the parking lot, where Joe's dark-blue Silverado was parked next to Riley's silver one. But his friend just gave a wave goodbye as Riley slid behind the truck's wheel and backed out of the parking lot.

He drove west, toward the small farmhouse located on the last parcel of what used to be his family's cattle ranch a couple of miles outside the Canyon Creek town limits. But he passed the house and kept driving west.

HANNAH WOKE TO SILENCE, her heart pounding. She lay in an unfamiliar bed, the unmistakable smell of antiseptic surrounding her. Her eyelids felt heavy and swollen, but she forced them open.

The room around her was mostly dark, only a faint sliver of light peeking under the door. A darkened television sat on a wall mount in one corner of the room. Curtained windows lined the wall beside her bed.

She was in the hospital, she remembered. She'd been attacked on the roadside and crashed while escaping. The memories returned in bright, painful fragments.

She lifted her hand to her face. The touch of her fingers to her raw skin hurt a little, though not as much as the dull ache settling in the center of her forehead. She touched the left side of her head and found a bandage there. From the wreck or from the man's attempt to slam her head into the steering wheel? Pressing lightly, she felt a sharp sting.

And how had she gotten away? She couldn't remember—

The door to the room opened, admitting a shaft of light from the hallway and the compact frame of a woman in blue scrubs. The woman crossed to her bed and pushed a button on the wall. The room filled with gentle golden light, giving Hannah a better look at her visitor.

She looked to be in her late forties, short and muscular, with sandy-brown hair and large blue eyes. A badge clipped to her belt read Lisa Raines, LPN. She smiled at Hannah as she reached for her wrist to check her pulse. "How're you feeling, Hannah?"

"Head hurts," Hannah croaked, her throat feeling raw.

"You took a bit of a bump. You have a concussion." She said it with a slight chuckle.

"You've told me that before, huh?" Hannah shifted into a sitting position, groaning a little as the room spun around her.

"Yeah, you had a little short-term memory loss when you first got here, so you kept asking the same questions every few minutes." Lisa slipped a blood-pressure cuff over Hannah's arm. "You're going to be fine, though. We didn't find anything seriously wrong. We're just going to keep you overnight for observation." Lisa checked her blood pressure and took her temperature, jotting notes on her chart. "Everything's looking normal. You must have a hard head."

"Has anyone called my family?"

"You didn't have any emergency contact information in your belongings. I can make a call for you if you like."

Hannah started to shake her head no but thought better of it. She'd told her mother she'd call once she reached Jackson Hole, just to check in. If her mother didn't hear from her soon, she might send half of her brothers north to Wyoming to find her. "Could I make the call myself?"

"Sure." Lisa smiled and waved her hand toward the phone by the bedside. "I'll be back in an hour to check on you again, but if you need me before then, just push the call button."

Hannah waited for Lisa to leave before she picked up the phone and dialed her parents' number. Her father picked up after a couple of rings.

"Hi, Dad, it's me. I'm in Jackson." Her voice came out much hoarser than she had intended.

"Hannah?" Her father sounded instantly suspicious. "What's wrong with your voice?"

She couldn't lie, now that he'd asked a direct question. "I had an accident."

"Are you okay? Where are you calling from?"

"The hospital, but I'm okay. I promise. Nothing broken. Just a concussion, but the nurse just told me I'm doing great and I'll be getting out of here in the morning. Can I speak to Mom a moment?"

A moment later, Beth Cooper took the phone. "Tell me everything that happened."

Settling back against the bed pillows, Hannah told her mother about the attack and her escape, trying not to make it sound too alarming. But by the time she was finished, her mother was making plans to fly to Wyoming immediately.

Tears stinging her eyes, Hannah fought the unexpected urge to agree. "Mom, there's no need to come up here. I'm okay, I promise. No real harm done, except to my rental car, and that's insured. I'm going to finish out my vacation just like I planned and I'll be home by Sunday evening."

"That's crazy. You get on a plane tomorrow and come home."

The temptation to do what her mother asked alarmed Hannah. The youngest of seven, and the only girl, she'd fought hard to assert herself, to prove she could take care of herself. The last thing she needed to do now was slink home to hide beneath her family's wings. She'd done enough of that over the past four years.

"No, I'm staying here, Mom. I need to do it."

Her mother was silent for a moment before she answered. "Okay. You're right. But you'll call me every night. Fair enough?"

Hannah smiled. "Fair enough."

"You're a brave woman," her mother said, her voice tinted with admiration.

"I had a good role model." Hannah blinked back hot tears. She heard the door handle to her hospital room rattle. The door started to open. "Looks like the nurse is back, so I need to go." She rang off and hung up the phone, turning back to face the nurse, ready to make a joke about how hard it was to get any sleep in a hospital.

But she stopped short as her visitor entered the soft cocoon of light surrounding her bed, revealing a pair of long, jean-clad legs and a shiny silver belt buckle.

Her heart rate doubling in the span of a second, she opened her mouth and screamed.

Chapter Two

At the sound of Hannah Cooper's scream, Riley whipped around to look behind him, half-certain he'd see a crazed maniac with a gun. But all he saw was a nurse run into the room, alarm in her eyes. She pushed past Riley to her patient's side.

"Who is he?" Hannah asked the nurse, gazing at Riley with wide, frightened eyes.

The nurse looked at him over her shoulder, her expression wary. "What are you doing here? Visiting hours are over."

"I'm sorry. I should have announced myself at the nurses' station." He hadn't done so, of course, because he didn't want anyone to tell him he couldn't see Hannah Cooper. "I'm Riley Patterson with the Canyon Creek Police Department. I wanted to talk to Ms. Cooper about what happened to her this afternoon."

"The police have already spoken to her." The nurse lifted her chin, looking like a she-wolf guarding her young.

"That was the Teton County Sheriff's Department," Riley said, not ready to give up until he'd talked to the victim alone. "I want to talk to her about a similar case in my jurisdiction." That was stretching the truth a bit; none of the murders he'd been looking into over the past three years had actually happened in the Canyon Creek jurisdiction. But if nobody else in Wyoming gave a damn about connecting the dots, he was happy to make it a Canyon Creek priority.

"What do you want to know?" Hannah Cooper spoke in a raspy drawl, her voice a combination of honey and steel. Her green eyes remained wide and wary, and she hunkered deeper into the pillow behind her as he approached, but her jaw squared and she didn't turn away when he reached her bedside.

"I'm going to reach into my pocket and show you my badge first." He kept his voice low and calm. "So you'll know I am who I say I am."

She remained wary as he showed her his credentials. "The guy who attacked me was driving a cop car." Her gaze lifted defiantly to his. "You'll forgive me if I'm not particularly impressed by your badge."

Of course. He should have considered that possibility. Sliding the badge into the back pocket of his jeans, he did his best to soften his expression. "I'm sorry. I know you've been through a terrible ordeal. If you want to call the Canyon Creek Police Department, they can verify my credentials—"

"That's not necessary." Anger flashed in her eyes, although he got the feeling she was angrier at herself than at him. She pushed her hair away from her face, taking a deep breath. When she spoke again, she was calmer. "It's okay, I don't mind talking to him for a minute," she told the nurse.

The nurse slanted a look at Riley, as if she wanted to argue, but after a short nod, she left them alone.

"I apologize for barging in without any warning." Riley pulled a chair next to her bed. "How are you feeling?"

"Like I've been kicked in the head and dipped in acid."

"Pepper spray's nasty." He'd been exposed a few times, mostly in his police training. "And so's a concussion. I took a hit my senior year playing football. Kept asking the trainer what had happened every other minute for a solid half hour."

His confession elicited a tiny smile from her, the effect dazzling. Bandages, blotchy skin and red-rimmed eyes disappeared, revealing how pretty she was beneath her injuries. Her eyes were a mossy-green, her pupils rimmed by a shock of amber—cat's eyes, bright and a little mysterious. Her small, straight nose and wide, full lips might have been dainty if not for her square, pugnacious jaw. She was a scrapper. He'd known a few scrappers in his life.

Her smile faded, and he felt a surprising twinge of disappointment. Her chin dipped when she spoke. "You said there was a similar case in your jurisdiction?"

He cleared his throat. "Actually, there are a handful of cases I've been looking at over the past three years. Similar MO's—women driving alone on the highway, incapacitated by pepper spray." He didn't add that they usually ended up dead, wrapped in plastic sheeting in some river or lake not far from the highway where they disappeared.

Her expression darkened. "How many got away like I did?"

He licked his lips and didn't answer.

She nodded slowly. "I'm lucky, aren't I?"

"Yeah, you are."

She took a deep breath, coughing a little from the aftereffects of the pepper-spray attack. Her lower lip trembled a moment, but she regained control, her gaze lifting to meet his. "He tried to pull me out of the car, but I kept hearing my brother's voice in my head. 'Don't let him get you out of the car.' So I smashed my elbow against his hand where it was sitting on the window frame and I drove off as fast as I could."

"That was smart and brave."

"I don't know about that," she said faintly. "I just didn't want to die today."

The simple emotion in her voice tugged at his gut. Had Emily felt that way, trapped by a monster on the highway out of Casper? He knew from the autopsy that she'd fought him— her fingernails had been ripped in places, and there was some pre-mortem bruising from the struggle. Had the pepper spray incapacitated her more than it had Hannah Cooper? Had she lacked the opening that Hannah had to fight back and get away?

He rubbed his forehead, struggling against the paralyzing images his questions evoked. "I saw your statement to the Sheriff's Department. You didn't see your assailant's face?"

"No. I barely saw his midsection through the window before he hit me with the pepper spray. I didn't see much of anything after that. Just blurry images."

"You mentioned a silver belt buckle. Can you remember what was on it?"

Her brow furrowed with tiny lines of concentration. "I just know it was silver and there was a pattern to it, but I can't remember what it was. Maybe I didn't get a good look."

Though his instinct was to push her to remember more, he held his tongue. As frustrating as it was not to have all the answers right now, he reminded himself how lucky he was to have a living, breathing witness to the killer's MO. Maybe she'd remember more as the effects of the trauma wore off.

"You look tired," he said.

"Gee, thanks," she muttered, and he smiled.

Behind them came a knock, then the door opened just enough for the light from the corridor to silhouette the shape of a man. The hair on the back of Riley's neck rose. On instinct, he moved to put himself between Hannah and the visitor.

"Sorry to interrupt. I'm with hospital security. The nurse

thought I should check and see if everything's okay here." The security guard remained in the doorway, his shoulders squared and his hands at his side, close to the unmistakable outline of his weapon holster.

"Everything's fine," Hannah said firmly. "Thank you."

With a nod, the security guard closed the door behind him.

"Did the Teton County Sheriff's Department offer to post a guard outside your door?" Riley asked.

"Why? The guy who attacked me didn't know me. I was— what do y'all call it? A target of opportunity?"

She was right, but leaving her alone here in the hospital didn't sit well with him. The staff had shown they had her best interests at heart, but he couldn't shake the idea that the wily killer he'd been looking for over the past three years wouldn't be happy leaving behind a live victim. The more time Hannah had to remember details from the attack, the more valuable she was to the police—and dangerous to the killer.

He pushed to his feet, sensing she was running out of energy. She needed her rest, and they could pick up this conversation in the morning. "I'm heading out now. You get some sleep and don't worry about any of this, okay?"

She nodded, her eyelids already starting to droop.

He slipped out of the room and headed down the hallway toward the nurses' station, where the nurse he'd met previously was making notes in a chart behind the desk. She looked up, her expression turning stern. "You didn't stress her out, did you?"

"Is there a waiting area on this floor?" he asked.

The nurse pointed out a door a few feet down the corridor.

Riley entered the room, which was mostly empty, save for a weary-looking woman stretched out across an uncomfortable-looking bench in the corner. Riley grabbed a seat near the entrance, where he could keep an eye on the door.

He hadn't wanted to worry Hannah Cooper, but it had occurred to him that, target of opportunity or not, she'd seen the killer and lived to tell.

The son of a bitch wouldn't like that one bit.

ONE OF THE DIRTY LITTLE secrets of hospitals was how shoddy hospital security was, especially in a place like Jackson, Wyoming. Jackson Memorial Hospital had a single security camera trained on the main entrance and a few guards scattered throughout the hospital in case trouble arose. If you looked like you belonged and knew where you were going, nobody gave you a second look.

That's how it worked in institutions of all sorts.

He wasn't on duty that evening, but it was a piece of cake to enter right through the front door, wearing his work garb, without anyone lifting an eyebrow. Now, he had just one more job to do to cover his tracks, and then he'd finish what he'd come here to do.

He slipped inside the empty security office and closed the door behind him.

SHE DREAMED OF HOME, with its glorious vista of blue water, green mountains and cloud-strewn skies. The lake house where she'd spent her first eighteen years of life had been built by her father's hands, with lumber and stone from right there in Gossamer Ridge, Alabama. Though she'd lived on her own for almost eight years, the lake house remained home to her, a place of refuge and a source of strength.

She didn't feel as if she was dreaming at first, the setting and companions as familiar and ordinary as the sound of her own voice. Out on the water, her brother Jake was taking a fisherman on a guided tour of the lake's best bass spots.

Nearby, her brother J.D. worked on the engine of a boat moored in one of the marina berths, while his eleven-year-old son, Mike, shot a basketball through the rusty old hoop mounted on the weathered siding of the boathouse.

She basked in the sun on her skin and breathed in the earthy wildness of the woods and the water from her perch on the end of the weathered wooden pier. Her bare toes played in the warm water, drawing curious bluegills close to the surface before they darted back down to safety near the lake bottom.

Suddenly, the pier shook and creaked beneath her as footsteps approached from behind. She turned to look up at the visitor and met a pair of brilliant blue eyes gazing out from the chiseled-stone features of Riley Patterson.

"Wake up," he said. "You're in danger."

The dream images shattered, like a reflection in a pool displaced by a falling stone. She woke to the murky darkness of a hospital room filled with alien smells and furtive movements. A shadow shifted beside her in the gloom, and she heard the faint sound of breathing by her bed.

She froze, swallowing the moan of fear rising in her throat. *It's a nurse,* she told herself. *Only a nurse. In a minute, she'll turn on the light and check my pulse.*

But why hadn't the nurse left the door to the hallway open?

She felt the slightest tug on the IV needle in the back of her hand. Peering into the darkness, she caught the faint glint of the IV bag as it moved.

The intruder was putting something into her IV line.

Panic hammering the back of her throat, she swallowed hard and tried to keep her breathing steady, even though her lungs felt ready to explode. Slowly, quietly, she tugged the tube from the cannula in her right hand until she felt the cool drip of liquid spreading across the bed sheet under her arm. She had no idea where the nurse call button was, but it didn't matter anyway. She was too terrified to move again. The last thing she wanted to do was let the intruder know she was awake.

Instead, she focused on her breathing, keeping it slow and steady. In and out. Her heart was racing, her head was aching, but she kept breathing until she felt the intruder move away from her bedside. A moment later, the door to her room opened and the silhouette of a man briefly filled the shaft of light pouring inside. But he was gone before she got more than a quick impression of a solid, masculine build.

The door clicked closed and she jerked herself to a sitting position, groping for the nurse call button that hung by a cord from the side of her bed. She flicked the switch that turned on the bedside light and frantically pressed the call button.

A few seconds later, a woman's tinny voice came through the call-button speaker. "Yes?"

"Someone just came into my room and tried to put something in my IV line," she said, her voice shaking.

After a brief pause, the nurse's voice came through the speaker again. "I'll be right there."

A few seconds later, the door opened and a nurse hurried inside. She hit the switch by the door, flooding the room with light. Her brow furrowing, she looked at the tube Hannah had extracted from the cannula. "Are you sure someone was in here?" she asked, checking the IV bag.

"He was standing right there. He put something in that port thing." Hannah pointed toward the bright orange injection port positioned a few inches below the IV bag.

The nurse's frown deepened.

The door to the room whipped open and Riley Patterson entered, his tense blue eyes meeting Hannah's. "What's going on? I saw the nurse run in here—"

Hannah watched him close the distance between them, unsettled by how glad she was to see the Wyoming lawman again. The memory of her dream, of his quiet warning, flashed through her mind, and she felt the sudden, ridiculous urge to fling herself in his arms and thank him for saving her life.

Instead, she murmured, "I thought you went home."

"You thought wrong," he said drily. "What happened?"

She told him what she'd just experienced, watching with alarm as his expression darkened. "I wasn't imagining it," she said defensively.

He looked at her. "I didn't say you were."

"I'll call security," the nurse said, heading for the door.

"I think we should call the Teton County Sheriff's Department, too." Riley reached for the phone.

"So you believe me?" Hannah pressed.

"Any reason I shouldn't?" He started dialing a number.

Hannah sank back against her pillows, reaction beginning to set in. She tried to hold back the shivers, but it was like fighting an avalanche. By the time Riley hung up the phone and turned around, her teeth were chattering wildly.

He sat beside her on the bed and took her hands in his. "It's okay. You're going to be okay."

His eyes were the color of the midday sky, clear and brilliant blue. They were a startling spot of color in his lean, sunbronzed face. He seemed hewn of stone, his short-cropped hair the rusty color of iron ore, his shoulders as broad and solid as a block of granite. His lean body could have been chiseled from the rocky outcroppings of the Wyoming mountains. He had cowboy written all over him.

Aware she was staring, she looked down at his hands enveloping hers. They were large, strong and work-roughened. A slim gold band encircled his left ring finger.

She tugged her hands away, acutely aware of her own bare ring finger. "I should have screamed. I let him get away."

"There are probably security cameras around. He took a big risk coming after you here."

"He was so calm." She gripped the bed sheets to keep her traitorous fingers from reaching for his hands again, though she felt absurdly adrift without his reassuring touch. "His actions were furtive, but he didn't seem nervous."

"Did you see anything about him?"

"It was too dark. I saw his outline when he slipped out the door—definitely male."

"My size?"

She let her gaze move a little too slowly over his hard, lean frame. Chiding herself mentally, she shook her head. "Heavier. More muscle-bound or something. Probably your height, maybe an inch or two taller." She pressed her lips together to stop her chattering teeth. "I should have made noise, gotten the nurses in here—"

"If you're right about what you saw, the man came here to kill you. Making a noise only would have made it happen faster." He briefly touched her hand where the cannula remained, unattached to the IV tube. "You got that tube out. You saved yourself, and nobody could expect anything more."

He was saying all the right things, but she heard disappointment in his voice. Clearly, finding the man who'd attacked her was more than just another case to him.

She'd always been insanely curious—nosy, her brothers preferred to call it—but something kept her from asking any more questions of Riley Patterson. She sensed that pushing him for more information would make him back off. She couldn't afford for him to back off.

A man had tried to kill her twice in one day, and she had a feeling Riley Patterson might be the only person who could stop him if he tried it a third time.

JOE GARRISON ARRIVED not long after the Teton County Sheriff's Department detectives. Riley caught his boss's eye as he entered Hannah Cooper's room, motioning him over with a twitch of his head. Joe met him in the corner, his gaze wandering across the small room to where Hannah Cooper sat in a chair by her empty bed, her green-eyed gaze following the activity of the evidence techs who were processing the scene.

"The Teton County Sheriff's Department wants her in protective custody, but she's refusing," Riley said. "She said she'd rather go home early tomorrow and forget all about this."

"You don't want her to leave."

Riley met his friend's understanding gaze. "She saw the guy. Maybe she didn't see his face, but she's the only living witness, and she's about to fly back home to Alabama."

"You can't keep her here against her will."

Riley pressed his hands against his gritty eyes. "I can't let her leave."

Joe's answer was dry as a desert. "So kidnap her and hold her hostage."

Riley slanted a look at his boss. "Did you drive all the way here to give me a hard time or are you going to help me figure out how to keep her in Wyoming?"

"Do you want me to arrest her or something?"

"Could we?" Riley glanced at Hannah, only half-joking. She looked calm now, more curious than worried, her slim fingers playing absently with the hem of her hospital gown, tugging it down over her knees.

"Maybe you should tell her why you're so desperate to solve this case."

Riley looked back at Joe. "Tell her about Emily?"

Joe nodded.

Riley looked at Hannah again and found her returning his gaze. After a couple of seconds, she looked away.

"Maybe if she knew how many victims we could be talking about, and the way they were killed…" Riley said softly.

"You want to scare her into staying?"

"Maybe she'll want to help."

Joe arched one eyebrow. "At the risk of her own life?"

Riley sighed. "You're just a wellspring of optimism."

"You want a yes man, you called the wrong guy." Joe thumped Riley on the arm. "But maybe you're right. The Teton County Sheriff's Department doesn't know what we know about these murders. They're not giving her the whole picture. I guess you could lay the truth on her and let her make an informed choice." Joe's gaze shifted as the hospital-room door opened and a tall, rangy lawman entered. "There's Jim Tanner."

As Joe left Riley to greet the Teton County Sheriff, Riley crossed to the chair where Hannah sat. She looked up at him, a dozen questions swirling behind her eyes. He smiled slightly and crouched beside her. "Three-ring circus."

"I'll be glad to be out of it," she admitted. "I get the feeling the police aren't taking me very seriously. I think they think I'm just paranoid."

"It shouldn't take that long to find out what the guy put in your IV tube. I heard them say the lab is working on it right now."

"They just want to prove it was nothing so they can pat me on the head and tell me it was just a dream."

Riley had a feeling she was right. "I don't think it was just a dream."

She shot him a look of pure gratitude. "I wasn't asleep. I know what I saw. And all that's supposed to be in that IV is saline, so there's no reason for anyone to put anything else into it."

"You don't have to convince me."

She lowered her voice, eyeing the technician standing nearby. "Nobody in the Teton County Sheriff's Department said anything about multiple murders."

He couldn't hold back a little smile. "Yeah, I know."

"But you disagree?"

He lowered his voice, too. "I've been tracking a series of murders, one or two a year, for the last three years. All across Wyoming, east to west, north to south. Women driving alone, disappearing en route from one place to another. Their bodies are later found wrapped in plastic, dumped in a lake, river or other body of water. Three of the six showed traces of pepper spray around the mouth, nose and eyes. The other bodies had too much weather exposure to take a sample."

Hannah's face went pale, but she didn't look away. "If I hadn't gotten away—"

He didn't finish the thought for her. He didn't need to.

The door to the room opened, and a woman in a white coat entered, carrying a file folder. She crossed to speak to Jim Tanner, whose brow furrowed deeply the longer she spoke. Joe looked across the room at Riley, his expression grim. Riley's stomach twisted into a knot.

Joe and Sheriff Tanner crossed to Hannah's side. Riley stood to face them.

"The lab report on the IV tube is back," Tanner said.

"And?" Hannah asked.

His expression grew hard. "There was enough digoxin in that tube to kill you in a matter of minutes."

Chapter Three

The buzz of urgent conversation surrounding her seemed to fade around Hannah as she took in Sheriff Tanner's quiet announcement.

Her attacker had tried to kill her. Again.

It had to be the same guy, right? It wasn't likely two different people would go after a nobody tourist like her. But why? She hadn't even seen him, really. She could remember almost nothing about him. Why did he consider her a threat?

She looked around for Riley Patterson, the closest thing to a familiar face in the room. His ice-blue eyes met hers, his expression grim but somehow comforting. He crouched beside her again, one hand resting on her forearm. "You okay?"

She nodded quickly, forcing her chin up. "I just want to know how he could get to me so easily."

"So do we," Sheriff Tanner assured her. "I've sent a man to check with hospital security. But I don't have much hope. This is a small hospital, and Jackson Hole's a pretty laid-back place. There's not much security in place here."

"He thinks he's invincible," Riley said softly. "He's gotten away with everything so far."

"Joe tells me you two think this attack is connected to other murders in the state," Sheriff Tanner said.

Riley glanced at Hannah. She could tell he didn't want to talk about this in front of her. He hadn't given her many details about the other cases he'd been investigating, though what he'd told her had been horrifying enough.

"I've made file folders full of notes," he told Sheriff Tanner. "I don't mind sharing. The more people looking for this guy, the better."

The Teton County sheriff studied Riley, his eyes narrowed, then turned his gaze to the lanky, dark-haired man Riley had introduced as his boss, Joe Garrison. "You vouch for this, Garrison?"

Joe nodded. "Riley's right. This guy has struck before, and he'll do it again if we don't stop him."

Sheriff Tanner didn't look happy to hear Joe's affirmation. "Okay, send me copies of your notes, and I'll put a detective on it. See if we can't tie it to any open cases we're working on."

"Cold cases, too. I've only been keeping notes since three years ago, but I think it could go back further," Riley said.

"Why three years ago?" Hannah asked.

Joe and Sheriff Tanner both turned to look at Riley, but Riley kept his eyes on Hannah, his expression mask-like.

When he didn't answer, she rephrased the question. "You said you've been keeping notes for only three years. What happened to make you start?"

Riley held her gaze a long moment, then looked down at his hands. He flexed his left hand, the ring on the third finger glinting as it caught the light. He spoke in a soft, raspy voice. "Three years ago, the son of a bitch murdered my wife."

Riley's words felt like a punch to Hannah's gut. No wonder he seemed personally involved in this case. "I'm sorry."

He acknowledged her condolences with a short nod, his mouth tightening. "I want this guy caught even more than you do," he added softly, as if the words were meant for her ears alone.

She swallowed hard, remembering how just a little while ago, she wanted nothing more than to catch the next plane home to Alabama. A part of her still did.

She'd done a lot of running home over the last four years.

But knowing what she now knew, could she really run away? She was possibly the only living witness who could identify a cold-blooded murderer.

A murderer who'd killed Riley Patterson's wife.

"Excuse me?"

Hannah turned at the sound of a new voice. The doctor who'd treated her in the Emergency Room when she arrived at the hospital stood nearby, his expression concerned.

"I'd like to check on my patient," he said firmly.

Riley stepped between the doctor and Hannah. "Mind if I see your ID?"

The look on the doctor's face almost made Hannah laugh. "Mind if I see yours?"

Riley had his badge out before the request was finished. The doctor's mouth quirked. Once he'd studied Riley's credentials, he held out his name tag for Riley's inspection. "James Andretti," he said aloud. "I've been working here for ten years. Ask anyone."

"He treated me in the E.R." Hannah touched Riley's arm. He retreated, though he didn't look happy about it.

"I'd like to check on my patient," Dr. Andretti repeated, giving Riley a pointed look. "Can you clear the room?"

"It's a crime scene," Riley said.

"It's also a hospital room."

Sheriff Tanner stepped in. "The techs have processed the areas around the bed. We'll step out a few minutes and let the doctor do his business. When he's done, I'll be back in to talk to you, Ms. Cooper."

Hannah gave a nod, darting a look at Riley. She found his gaze on her, his expression impossible to read. But when the other police personnel left her room, he followed, leaving her alone with the doctor.

Dr. Andretti pulled out his stethoscope and bent to listen to Hannah's heart through her hospital gown. "Heart rate's a little elevated, but I guess that's to be expected. How's your head feeling?"

"Better, actually," Hannah admitted. The headache that had plagued her earlier in the evening had faded to nothing.

He had her follow his fingers as he moved them in front of her face. "No double vision, no more memory lapses?"

"Nope."

"Good. Looks like we'll spring you in the morning. But I think we should move you to another room so you can get some rest."

"Do I really need to be here at all?" she asked.

"That's how we usually handle a concussion."

"But I'm not symptomatic anymore, right? You only kept me for observation and you just said I'm doing fine."

The doctor shot her a questioning look.

"Somebody's already gotten to me here tonight. I'm not that comfortable hanging around to let them have another shot."

"I can have a security guard posted at your door."

"You don't know one of your guards isn't behind this. Or even another doctor or nurse," she pointed out.

Dr. Andretti bristled visibly. "That's not likely."

Hannah sighed. "Maybe not. I just want to get out of here. I don't have to have your permission to check out, do I?"

"No—"

"Then arrange it. Please."

"What are you going to do when you leave? It's four in the morning. No motels worth staying in are going to let you check in at this hour. Assuming you can even find a room available."

"I just want out of here." A tingle of panic was beginning to build in the center of her chest. The thought of staying in this room until the next day was unbearable.

"Why don't I go get the nice police officers to tell you why leaving right now would be a very big mistake?" Dr. Andretti suggested, making a final note in her chart and tucking it under his arm. "You stay put."

He left her alone in the hospital room, which now looked like a war zone, thanks to the handiwork of the evidence technicians. She tucked her knees up to her chin and closed her eyes, feeling as tired as she could ever remember. But she couldn't afford to fall asleep.

Not in this place, surrounded by people she didn't know and couldn't trust.

"SIX MURDERS DON'T SEEM like much over three years," Jim Tanner said, passing Riley a cup of lukewarm coffee from the half-empty carafe on the break-room hotplate. "I thought serial murderers tend to escalate, but this guy's pretty steady at two a year."

"Well, Hannah would have been three this year." Riley grimaced at the taste of the stale coffee.

"So he's escalating…slowly?" Tanner looked skeptical.

"There may be others. These are the ones I've been able to glean from relatively public sources."

"You'd think the feds would be all over this."

"Some of the links are nebulous," Joe said, refusing Tanner's offer of coffee. "We've only linked three of the murders to pepper-spray attacks. Two years ago there were two instances, and one last year. And what happened to Hannah."

"All six of the murder victims were wrapped in plastic sheeting and dumped in bodies of water," Riley pointed out. "All six were killed by ligature strangulation."

"That's not an unusual mode of murder. Same ligature used each time?"

"No," Riley admitted. "I think he uses weapons of opportunity."

"Victims of opportunity, weapons of opportunity—" Tanner shook his head. "Yeah, I could see the FBI needing more."

Riley glanced at Joe. Did his old friend secretly agree with Jim Tanner and the FBI about the scarcity of connections between the cases? Was he simply humoring Riley out of loyalty?

Tanner put his cup down on the Formica counter. "You know what? You clearly believe the cases are linked, and I'm not one to blow off a fellow cop who's having a hunch. I'll put one of my guys on the cold cases in our jurisdiction, see if any of them match any of your criteria. Maybe it'll help flesh out the body of evidence. You never know."

Riley gave the Teton County chief a grateful half smile. "I appreciate it."

"Sheriff Tanner?"

Riley turned and saw Hannah's doctor approaching, a frown creasing his forehead.

"Can I help you?" Tanner asked.

"Ms. Cooper is asking to leave the hospital early. Now, in fact. She feels uncomfortable remaining here."

Riley's stomach tightened. "Did you leave her alone?"

"I posted a guard outside, but—"

Riley didn't wait for the rest of his sentence, pushing past Joe and heading back to Hannah's room. He didn't see a guard outside her door, or any other door lining the corridor.

His heart rate climbing, Riley pushed open the door to Hannah's room and almost bumped into the guard standing just inside. He was a slim man in his early twenties, with crow-black hair and sun-bronzed skin. He was laughing as he turned to look at Riley.

Riley pushed past him, putting himself firmly between the guard and Hannah. "Are you okay?" he asked her, keeping his eyes on the guard, whose brow furrowed at Riley's question.

"I'm fine. Charlie was just introducing himself, since he was going to be my babysitter." Humor and annoyance tinted Hannah's whiskey drawl. "I was just telling him I'm thinking of digging a tunnel out."

Riley arched an eyebrow at the guard. "Shouldn't you be frisking me or something? Checking my ID?"

Charlie looked suitably crestfallen.

"He's messing with you," Hannah said. "Riley, leave him alone."

"Go stand guard outside and don't let anyone in without checking ID," Riley told the younger man, his tone firm. Charlie quickly obeyed.

Riley turned to look at Hannah, who still sat in the chair by the window. Her knees were tucked up against her chest, her chin resting atop them as she gazed at him with sleepy green eyes. He felt a funny twisting sensation in his gut. "You look wiped out."

"Always with the compliments," she said around a yawn. "Your doctor says you want out of here."

"Ya think?"

He managed a smile at the crack. "There won't be any flights out before 8:00 a.m. What do you plan to do, camp out in the airport where you don't know a soul?"

"I'm camped out in a hospital where I don't know a soul. At least at the airport I wouldn't be wearing a cotton smock with an open back."

There was a quiet knock on the hospital-room door, and a moment later, Joe Garrison and Jim Tanner entered, followed by one of the Teton County evidence technicians holding a notebook computer.

"Trammell here has a copy of the only security-camera footage available," Tanner said, motioning for Trammell to set up the notebook computer on the over-bed table at the foot of the hospital bed. "I want you to watch and see if anyone looks familiar."

"I didn't get a good look at him either time."

"You can at least eliminate people by body type. It can't hurt."

Riley and Joe gathered around the computer as Trammell hit play. Riley felt a prickle of warmth down the left side of his body and turned to find Hannah sitting closer to him, like a kitten curling up next to a heat source. The mental image amused him.

He reached behind her to grab the blanket wadded near the foot of the bed and caught a glimpse of golden skin peeking out the back of her hospital gown.

She smiled her appreciation when he tucked the blanket around her, then turned back to the computer. "What are we looking at?" she asked Trammell.

"This is the front entrance." Trammell pointed to a pair of glass doors center frame. "We asked for everything from about an hour before you arrived to the time you called the nurse's station around 1:00 a.m." He pointed to another button. "Click that button and it'll fast-forward the images. Click that one and it'll pause the image."

It was easy to fast-forward the video; about half the visitors could be eliminated by their sex, others by age or build. Hannah stopped the video three times, but each time she shook her head. "I don't think so."

Riley frowned, something on the video catching his eye. "The hell?" He reached across and hit the pause button, then touched another to reverse the video.

"What is it?" Hannah asked.

"I'm not sure—" He saw the flicker again and hit pause.

"Oh," Hannah said, her voice tinted with surprise.

On the screen, the tip of one dark boot was visible just past the edge of the mottled carpet in front of the lobby door.

"Well, hell." Tanner grimaced at the screen.

"Someone tampered with the recording." Riley looked at Joe, whose blue eyes had darkened.

"Son of a bitch," Jim Tanner growled.

"How did he manage that?" Hannah asked.

Riley laid his hand on her shoulder. She gave a little trembling jerk, turning her head to look up at him. He gave her shoulder a squeeze and felt her relax under his touch.

Tanner released a deep sigh and turned to look at them. "Inside job?"

Joe nodded. "Probably. It's where I'd start looking for sure."

"But why would someone who worked here want to hide his image? It's not like it would raise an alarm," Hannah said.

"Unless they tampered with the image to throw us off," Riley countered. As convoluted as that possibility sounded, he wouldn't put it past their target to be just that devious.

"I'll get a list of all the personnel, then. Security, medical staff, sanitation, the whole lot." Tanner clapped his technician on the shoulder. "Trammel, I want the original footage sent to the crime lab in Cheyenne. See if those fellows can get anything out of it."

Trammell nodded, grabbed his computer and left.

Tanner looked at Hannah. "I think you're right, Ms. Cooper. It's not a good idea for you to stay here tonight. I can set you up in protective custody here in Jackson—"

Hannah turned and looked at Riley. "You said I'm the only one who ever got away."

"That we know of," Riley agreed.

"I'm the only one who's seen him." Her voice softened even more. She moved away from them, toward the window, her arms wrapped around her as if she felt a sudden chill. The movement spread the back of her hospital gown even wider, baring more of the golden skin on her back and the sweet curve of her bottom beneath the cotton of her pale-blue panties.

Riley felt a flutter low in his belly and clamped his teeth together, surprised by his body's traitorous response. He cleared his throat and glanced at Joe and Jim Tanner. Both men were looking at him rather than Hannah's pretty backside, which made him feel like even more of a slug.

"Have you talked to her doctor?" Joe asked Tanner in a faint murmur. "What are the chances of her getting back more memories of the attack?"

"Nobody knows," Tanner admitted. "Head injuries are unpredictable. She might never remember anything more than she's told us."

"There might not be anything more to remember," Joe said grimly. "I hoped when we learned there was a living witness—"

"We know a lot more than we did," Riley pointed out,

glancing at Hannah again. She'd turned and was watching them whisper among themselves, her eyes slightly narrowed.

"I'm still here in the room," she said aloud, making the other men look at her as well. "Since I'm pretty sure you're talking about me, why don't y'all tell me what's on your minds?"

Riley walked toward her slowly. "We were discussing what you do and don't remember about the attack."

"Not much," she admitted, her voice apologetic. "I'd hoped that I'd remember more once the symptoms of the concussion passed, but I come back to the same thing. I didn't get a good look at him when he pulled me over. I remember jeans and a silver belt buckle. He seemed fit—muscular, or at least that's the impression I got before he sprayed me in the face with pepper spray. It happened so fast."

Riley touched her shoulder again. "You told us he posed as a cop. That's something we didn't know before, and I think it could be important." If nothing else, it suggested the man might have some law-enforcement experience, or at least more understanding of police work than the average citizen.

"What if it's not enough?" Hannah asked. "What if I fly out of here tomorrow and nothing changes? What if he goes on killing people?"

Riley frowned, not following. "We keep looking for him anyway."

She looked up at him suddenly, her green eyes bright with an emotion he couldn't identify. "I'm the only living witness. If I leave—"

She didn't finish the sentence, but Riley finally understood what she was getting at. "If you leave, it could hamper the investigation," he admitted aloud.

Her head lowered, her back slumping as if it suddenly bore a terrible weight. Riley felt a rush of pity for her, for he had some idea of what she was feeling. It was a horrible thing, carrying the burden of six unsolved murders, knowing that it fell on you to bring them justice and closure.

"I can't leave Wyoming, can I?" she asked softly.

He didn't answer, knowing it was a question she had to answer herself.

Her tongue ran lightly over her lips and he saw her throat bob as she swallowed. When she looked up at him again, her gaze was solemn but direct. "I have five more days left of my vacation. I can't stay forever, but I can give you those five days. Maybe it'll be enough."

"We can put you in protective custody," Jim Tanner offered.

"She needs to go somewhere the killer doesn't expect her to be." Riley glanced at Joe.

"Somewhere small and off the beaten path?" Joe asked, his voice faintly dry.

Riley shrugged and turned back to Hannah. "Canyon Creek is about an hour and a half from here, in ranching country. I have a place there. Plenty of room. Great view."

Hannah's brow creased. "You want me to stay alone with you? I don't even know you."

"You don't have to know me. You just have to trust me."

The room fell silent as Hannah considered his words. The walls seemed to close in around them, every molecule, every atom focused on her words.

He wasn't sure what he wanted her answer to be, now that he'd made the offer. He'd lived alone for three years, his home both a refuge and a prison since Emily's death. He'd found a certain familiar comfort in his loneliness, Emily's absence so powerful it became a tangible thing he could hold on to when the nights were dark and long. He hadn't let anyone intrude on his solitude in a long time.

Hannah would change that. How could she not?

Hannah released a long, deep breath and looked up at them. "Okay."

Riley felt as if the ground was crumbling beneath his feet.

"Let's do it," she said, her chin high. "Let's go to Canyon Creek."

Chapter Four

"Joe shouldn't have dragged you out of bed to do this." Hannah took the blanket Jane Garrison handed her, feeling terrible about putting a stranger—a pregnant stranger—through so much trouble.

"I wasn't asleep. I'm not used to my husband being called to Jackson in the middle of the night." Jane's expression was a mixture of ruefulness and besottedness. Clearly, she was madly in love with Canyon Creek's Chief of Police.

"I guess it's usually quiet around here, huh?" Hannah had dozed a bit on the drive from Jackson, drained from the last eventful hours, but she'd awakened long enough to see that Riley Patterson's small ranch house was located smack dab in the middle of Nowhere, Wyoming. He had assured her there was a town a few miles to the east, with stoplights and everything, but they were clearly in ranch country, where the closest neighbors—the Garrisons, as it turned out—were six miles down a narrow one-lane road.

"Quiet?" Jane's lips quirked. "Mostly, yes. But we do have our moments, now and then." She crossed to the corner, where an old-fashioned wood stove sat silent and cold, and started to pick up pieces of firewood from a nearby bin.

"Let me do that." Hannah quickly intervened.

"You have a concussion," Jane protested.

"And you're pregnant," Hannah countered firmly.

Jane gave her an exasperated look. "It's not a disease."

Hannah laughed. Jane's lips curved and she finally gave into laughter as well.

"Joe treats me like I'm suddenly made of glass when he knows damned well I'm tough as old leather," Jane complained as she opened the door to the stove so Hannah could throw some wood inside. "I've lived through the Wyoming winter for two years now. Having a baby's nothing compared to that."

"I wouldn't say it's nothing." Hannah put the last piece of wood on the fire and stepped back. "How does this thing work? We're more into air-conditioning where I live."

Jane took over lighting the wood stove. "You're from Alabama?"

Hannah sat on the end of the bed, watching Jane's deft hands strike a match to the kindling she'd piled atop the stack of wood inside the iron stove's belly. "Yeah. It's a little town called Gossamer Ridge, up in northeast Alabama. It's pretty small. My family owns a few hundred acres on Gossamer Lake. We run a marina and fishing camp there. Most of my brothers and I work there in some capacity."

"You have a lot of brothers?" Jane stepped back from the stove, holding her hands out to warm them from the radiant heat.

"Six. I'm the youngest and the only girl."

"Wow. Six brothers." Jane settled carefully in a rocker next to the bed, rubbing her hand over her round belly. "I'm an only child. Joe had a brother, but he died." For a second, Jane's expression grew bleak, her eyes dark with pain. She took a deep breath and seemed to physically shake off the sadness. "Riley's an only child, too. It can be lonely."

"He seems lonely." Hannah kicked herself mentally the second the words spilled from her lips. The last thing she should be doing was psychoanalyzing the man who'd made himself her guardian angel. She should just accept his offer of protection for what it was and try not to get any more involved.

She'd already made the mistake of falling for a guy who was hung up on another woman and lived to regret it. She had no intention of making the same mistake again.

But Jane wasn't ready to drop the subject, apparently. "He's a complicated guy."

"I know about his wife's death." And understood his thirst for justice better than he might have imagined. Her own brother, J.D., whose wife had been murdered several years ago, was still waiting for justice as well.

She wondered if either man would get what they wanted.

Jane gave her a sidelong look. "I didn't know Emily. She had died about a year before I met Joe. He tells me Riley used to be very different. Clowning around, always the one to crack a joke—" She stopped herself. "Like I said, complicated."

Hannah resisted the temptation to push for more information. She was here for only a few more days, and her focus needed to be on remembering the lost details of her ordeal with the fake cop, not on Riley Patterson's tragic past.

She quickly changed the subject. "Is this your first child?"

"Yeah." Jane rubbed her belly. "Joe keeps talking about lots of kids. I told him he can carry the rest of them."

Hannah grinned, deciding she liked Jane Garrison. She wasn't what you'd call pretty, exactly, with her freckle-spotted face and unruly brown curls, but her emerald eyes were full of life and laughter, and when she smiled, Hannah couldn't help smiling back.

"I missed my mother's pregnancies, being the youngest. But my brothers tell me stories that would curl your hair."

Jane chuckled. "Scooter here has been pretty good for most of the pregnancy, but now that I'm nearing the goal line, he's started kicking up a storm—"

"And you love it."

Riley's deep voice from the doorway drew Hannah's gaze. She felt suddenly, intensely aware of him as he entered the room, his boots thumping against the hardwood floor with each step. He'd shed the leather jacket and dress shirt for a dark-blue T-shirt. A sizzle of pure attraction shot through Hannah's body, settling low in her belly. It simmered there, spreading warmth through her veins.

She tamped it down ruthlessly. The last time she'd let her heart and hormones lead her head, she'd ended up heartbroken and humiliated.

"Joe's on the phone with Jim Tanner," Riley told Jane, holding out his hand to her. "He said to round you up and head you in the direction of the front door. You're supposed to be resting like a good mama-to-be."

Jane rolled her eyes. "See what I have to put up with?" But she let Riley help her from the rocking chair, and the look of affection she gave him when he ruffled her curls made Hannah smile. Jane waggled her fingers at Hannah. "Call if you need anything. Riley has our number."

"I will," Hannah agreed, though she didn't plan on imposing on the Garrisons or Riley if she could avoid it.

While Riley walked to the front of the house with Jane, Hannah pulled her suitcase onto the bed and started unpacking. The closet across from the bed was empty, save for a couple of extra blankets piled atop a high shelf. Hannah filled several of the bare clothes hangers with her sparse collection of blouses and sweaters. Jeans, T-shirts and underwear went into the small chest of drawers by the door.

Her toiletries she kept in the bag she'd packed them in, since she'd be sharing the house's only bathroom with Riley. She couldn't quite bring herself to store her deodorant next to his on the sink counter.

Riley tapped on the open door, making her jump. "Do you have everything you need?"

She looked up to find him leaning against the door frame, his arms folded over his chest. His direct gaze made the skin on the back of her neck prickle, but she refused to look away. If they were going to be sharing this house for the next few days, she was going to have to control her rattled nerves. Now was as good a time to start as any.

"I'm taking the rest of the week off from work," he told her, pushing away from the door and walking farther into the room. His broad shoulders and muscle-corded frame seemed to crowd the room, leaving Hannah feeling small and vulnerable. She stood up, thinking it would put them on more equal footing, but rising only brought her closer to him. Up close, he seemed bigger than she'd thought, solid, hard and masculine. He smelled good, a tangy combination of pine needles and sweet hay. He'd gone with Joe to check on the horses in the stable, she remembered, while Jane helped her settle in.

Taking a step backwards, she forced her thoughts back to what he'd just said. "Don't take time off on my account."

His lips quirked. "I have to. Since I'm supposed to be protecting you."

"I should be safe enough here by myself. The guy who attacked me doesn't know where to find you, does he?"

"I wouldn't think so. But I don't think we should take chances. I'm not really going to be off. This is police business."

To her relief, he backed away, settling in the rocker where Jane had sat earlier, his long legs stretched in front of him. "Joe's going to tell everyone he forced me to take vacation. They'll believe it. I haven't been off in a couple of years."

She arched her eyebrows. "Workaholic?"

His expression closed. "I just like to work."

She knew a warning flag when she saw one. She shifted the subject. "The doctor told me before I left that I could get back some of the memory that's hazy right now. About the day of the attack, I mean. Maybe I'll remember more about what the man was wearing—the belt buckle, what kind of shirt he had on."

"It's possible," he conceded. "Meanwhile, Jim Tanner is looking into the backgrounds of the hospital personnel."

"I don't know that just anyone would know how to tamper with a security camera." Hannah sat down cross-legged on the end of the bed, tucking her feet under the blanket Jane had given her. A cold wind had picked up during the night, blasting the valley with a bitter autumn chill that the little wood stove couldn't quite combat.

"There are a few ways it could have been done. The tech guys in Cheyenne will be able to tell us more." Riley shifted in his chair and pulled a cell phone from his pocket. "I want you using this to make all your calls. It's my personal cell phone. I can use my work phone. I don't want you to use your own phone while you're here in Wyoming."

She frowned. "Why not?"

"We don't know how much this guy knows about you now. If he's a hospital employee, he could have accessed your hospital records, which would give him a hell of a lot of personal information at his fingertips. If he has your cell phone number, he could possibly have a way to trace its use."

Hannah's stomach gave a little flip as she took the phone from him. "Are you trying to scare me or something? Believe me, it's not necessary."

"I just want you to be on guard every moment. Think about the things you do and say, who you talk to. I assume you'll want to call your family to let them know where you are?"

Hannah rubbed her head. She hadn't even thought about what she was going to tell her parents about what she'd decided to do. "I don't know what to tell them."

"It's up to you. Tell them as much or as little as you think they need to know."

"If I tell them too much, there'll be eight Coopers on the next flight to Wyoming."

"Tell them you met a nice doctor at the hospital and he's taking you skiing in Jackson Hole." Riley's lips quirked. "A nice rich doctor. Don't mothers love to hear stuff like that?"

"My mother can sniff out a lie faster than a bloodhound on a 'possum."

He grinned at that. "So tell her you met a nice cop who took you home and has you locked in his spare bedroom."

She rolled her eyes. "That's *so* much better."

His soft laugh caught her by surprise. It was a great laugh, musical and fluid, though it sounded a bit rusty, as if he hadn't used it in a while.

Maybe he hadn't.

"Just tell her the truth," he suggested, his laughter dying. "But don't make it sound too scary. I'm pretty sure the guy who attacked you hasn't yet connected you to me, so that should keep you safe while we see if we can put together all the pieces to our puzzle."

Hannah glanced at the clock sitting on the bedside table. It read 5:30 a.m. "Is that clock right?"

Riley checked his watch. "Yes."

It was an hour later in Alabama. Her parents would be up by now. She flipped open the cell phone he'd handed her and dialed her parents' number.

Her mother answered, sounding sleepy. "Hello?"

"Hey, Mom, it's me."

"What's wrong?"

Hannah smiled at her mother's immediate leap to the worst possible conclusion. "Everything's okay. I just wanted to let you know what's happening."

She caught her mother up to date on all that had happened, pausing now and then to allow her mother to catch her father up on all that she was saying. Feeling Riley's gaze on her, she looked up to find him studying her with slightly narrowed eyes. His hands rested on the arms of the rocker, his fingers drumming softly on the polished wood, but it seemed more a nervous twitch than a sign of impatience.

"You need to be on the next plane instead of holed up under police protection," her mother said firmly.

"I have almost a week left of my vacation, Mom. If I stick around, maybe something will trigger my memory—"

"You can trigger your memory in the safety of your own home," Beth Cooper insisted. "Mike, talk to your daughter."

"Mom—don't…Hi, Dad."

"You mother wants me to tell you to come home." Her father's gruff voice held a hint of weary amusement. "Of course, I know damned well you're going to do whatever you want, just like you have since you were six years old. Can you just promise you'll be careful?"

"I promise I'll be careful."

"Good. Now, can I talk to the policeman? Is he there with you now?"

Hannah's eyes widened with alarm. "Come on, Daddy, you don't need to talk to him—"

Across from her, one of Riley's eyebrows ticked upward. "Your father wants to talk to me?"

"Is that him?" Mike Cooper asked. "Hand him the phone."

With a deep sigh, Hannah held the phone out to Riley. "I'm sorry," she whispered, "but trust me, it's easier just to talk to him and get it over with."

Riley's lips twitched as he took the phone from her. "Hello, Mr. Cooper."

Hannah could hear the low rumble of her father's voice coming from the cell phone receiver, but she couldn't make out any words. There was no telling what he was telling Riley. She'd been present for enough pre-date lectures to know there was no way to predict what her father might say if he thought her welfare was at stake.

"Yes, sir, I absolutely will," Riley said a few minutes later. His eyes flickered up to meet hers. "Yes, I'm beginning to realize that."

"What did he just say about me?" she whispered, mortified.

"No, sir. I won't." Riley's smile spread slowly. "Oh, absolutely. You can count on me."

"Won't what? Count on you for what?" Hannah reached out for the phone. "Give that to me."

"Here she is again, sir." Riley handed over the phone, grinning. "Didn't get many second dates?" he whispered.

"No," she whispered back, before putting the phone to her ear. "Dad, I hope you didn't embarrass me."

"I just made sure your cowboy cop knows that we expect you back in Alabama by the end of the week alive and in one piece."

"I can do that by myself. Give Mom a kiss for me and I'll

call back tomorrow." To her horror, she felt tears burning the back of her eyes. "I need to get some sleep. Bye!"

She wiped at the tears with the back of her hand, but they just kept coming. She turned her face away from Riley, hating that one stupid little call home had made her turn into a blubbering baby.

She heard his boot steps moving out of the room and down the hall, no doubt to give her a little space to have a good cry without an audience. But a few seconds later, she heard him return. The bed shifted as he sat down next to her.

"Here." He thrust a small white handkerchief into her hand. "It's clean."

She laughed and used it to wipe her eyes. "Thank you. I'm sorry to act like such a baby."

"It's okay," he assured her. "Listen, it's been a long night, and I bet we both could use a little sleep. I'm going to make sure we're locked up tight and then I'll get a little shut-eye myself."

She twisted the handkerchief between her fingers. "I bet you don't usually lock up, do you?"

He looked at her. "No. Not usually."

"I don't lock up at home much, either. I guess that's craziness in a world like this, huh?" She tried to smile, but inside, she felt as if something small and innocent had died.

The bleak understanding she saw in his eyes was cold comfort. "I guess it is." He gave a brief nod and left the bedroom, closing the door behind him.

RILEY SLOWLY CIRCLED the ranch house, checking doors and windows to make sure they were secure. The place was all that was left of his family ranch—the house, the stable and enough acres of land for the horses to graze and roam. His parents had wearied of the bitter Wyoming winters and the struggle to make a cattle ranch thrive when family ranches were a dying breed. So they'd retired to Arizona.

They'd offered to let him keep more of the land, to turn the place into a guest ranch, like so many places in the state had become, but he liked his work as a cop, and Emily was dedicated to her nursing job. Plus, they'd been talking about starting a family. They couldn't have given any time to running a dude ranch.

So much had changed since then. His whole life, really.

He wandered into his bedroom and sat on the edge of the old four-poster bed Emily had found at a flea market in Thermopolis. It was solid oak, battered by time and use, but she'd loved it. He was a man, and it was a bed, so he'd loved it, too.

He'd loved her in it.

He released a weary breath and pulled his boots off, letting them drop to the floor with two heavy thuds. Stripping off his T-shirt, he lay back on the bed and closed his eyes, trying to will himself to sleep.

For the moment, Hannah Cooper was safe with him. Only a handful of people knew where she was going when she left the hospital—Joe, Sheriff Tanner and him. Tanner had agreed not to tell anyone else on the Teton County force.

But secrets had a way of getting out, no matter how carefully you tried keeping them, he knew. About a year earlier, he'd seen how easily a bad man with determination and the right connections could find the person he was looking for. Joe and Jane had nearly died as a result.

He didn't want Hannah Cooper to die because he was sleep deprived and off his game. He was so close to finding the bastard who'd killed Emily and destroyed his life.

He couldn't make any mistakes.

He pushed himself up from the bed and grabbed a fresh

change of clothes from the bureau by the bed. Maybe a shower would help him relax. He started out into the hall, then back-tracked to grab the Ruger pistol in its holster by his bed.

He paused in the bathroom doorway, listening for sounds from the guest room. Everything was quiet.

Too quiet?

He shook off the paranoid thought and entered the bathroom. He turned on the shower to let the water warm while he undressed, then stepped into the hot spray. The drum-beat of water felt good on his tense muscles.

Unbidden, an image popped into his mind. Hannah Cooper's bare back, smooth and golden-brown, peeking through the ribbons of her hospital gown. The thin cotton had done little to hide her curvy hips or the soft swell of her breasts.

He closed his eyes and pressed his head against the shower tiles, reaching down to turn the cold tap.

HANNAH HEARD THE SHOWER cut on and wished she'd thought of it first. She'd managed a sponge bath in the hospital, but a nice hot shower seemed like sheer bliss at the moment.

And maybe it would help her fall asleep, because lying here staring at the ceiling wasn't getting it done.

She sat up, lifting her hand to her brow as the room spun a little. Her equilibrium settled and she padded barefoot out of the bedroom to the kitchen just down the hall. She found a tumbler in the cabinet next to the sink and filled it with water from the tap. Leaning against the counter, she drained it quickly and turned back to the sink for a refill.

Behind her, she heard the rattle of a door lock. Her whole body jerked with reaction. The glass slipped from her nerve-less fingers and shattered in the sink.

The door opened behind her with a creak. Cool morning

air drifted inside, scattering chill bumps along her bare legs. Down the hall, the shower cut off.

Reaching into the sink, Hannah grabbed the bottom of the broken tumbler and whirled around to face the intruder, holding the jagged glass in front of her.

A tall, slim man with raven-black hair and dark eyes stared back at her, his mouth open with what looked like genuine surprise. "Who the hell are you?"

"Don't take another step!" Hannah said firmly as he started toward her.

He held up his hands and froze in place.

Down the hall, the bathroom door opened, slamming back against the wall. Riley burst into the kitchen, wearing nothing but a dark-blue towel and carrying a Ruger. He swept Hannah behind him and turned to face the intruder.

"Geez, cowboy, dial it down a notch," the dark-haired man drawled.

Riley's shoulders slumped, and he dropped the Ruger to his side. "Jack."

"Jack?" Hannah asked.

"Jack." The dark-haired man peeked over Riley's shoulder and waggled his fingers at her.

Riley laid the gun on the counter and stepped aside. He waved at Jack. "Hannah, this is Jack, my brother-in-law."

Jane had told her that Riley was an only child, so Jack must be...

"Emily's brother," Jack added, slanting a look at Riley.

Riley's lips pressed to a thin line. "I thought you were in Texas these days."

"Yeah, well, Texas had about all of Jack Drummond it could handle." Jack smiled wickedly at Hannah, flashing a pair of dimples Hannah was sure had broken more than one heart in Texas. Then he looked at Riley, his smile fading. When he next spoke, there was a dark undercurrent in his voice. "So, Riley—you've moved on, I see."

Riley looked at Hannah, his eyes dark with pain. "Had to happen some time. This is Hannah Cooper. My new girlfriend."

Hannah dropped the broken glass she'd been holding.

Chapter Five

"Don't move," Riley said quickly, putting out a warning hand toward her. "You're barefooted."

She met his urgent gaze, trying to regain her mental balance. Had he really just stormed in here, wearing nothing but a blue towel, and told his brother-in-law that she was his new girlfriend?

What the hell was he thinking?

A droplet of water slid down the side of his neck and pooled briefly in the hollow of his throat before trickling over the muscles of his chest. Hannah licked her lips and dragged her gaze away to meet Jack Drummond's dark scrutiny.

Now that her initial panic had subsided, she saw that Riley's brother-in-law was only a little older than she, no more than thirty. His sun-bronzed skin was smile-lined, as if he laughed a lot, although at the moment, the pained look in his eyes made her stomach hurt.

"I guess I shouldn't have just sprung the news on you like that, Jack. I wanted to be a little more sure where things were heading—" He shot Hannah a look full of pleading, as if begging her to play along with his story.

She cleared her throat. "I told him he should call you and

give you a heads-up." Her tone was more tart than she'd intended. "Small-town gossip. Things get around fast. But you know how he likes to do things his own way."

Jack crossed slowly to the kitchen table, his boots crunching over the shards from the glass she'd dropped. He sank into the nearest chair. "How long has it been going on?"

Hannah shot Riley another look. How was she supposed to answer that? They didn't have their stories straight yet.

"Let me get a broom and sweep this up." Riley disappeared down the hall, returning with a broom. He swept up the glass around her feet, clearing a path to the door. "Go get dressed and get some shoes on. I'll let Jack in on what's going on." He moved so close that she could feel the steamy heat of his damp skin. He smelled good, like fresh air and a hint of pine. Her hands curled into fists.

She tamped down the urge to bury her nose in his neck to breathe in more of that heady scent. "And then you'll let me in on it?" she added under her breath, soft enough that Jack couldn't hear.

He answered with an apologetic look and a quick gesture toward the guest bedroom.

She scurried down the hall to get dressed, keeping an ear cocked to follow the conversation going on in the kitchen as she pulled on a pair of jeans and a warm sweater.

There was a soft tinkle of glass—Riley sweeping up the glass she'd broken. "Out of minutes on your cell phone?" he asked drily.

"You and Emily never used to care if I called ahead." There was a petulant tone in Jack's voice that Hannah had not expected. She dropped her estimate of his age by a couple of years. "'Drop by anytime, Jack. We love to see you, Jack.'"

"You were her only family."

"And now you're my only family," Jack shot back. "At least, I thought you were."

Hannah paused in the middle of tying her shoe, the pang of sorrow in Jack Drummond's voice catching her by surprise. He sounded so sad. It made her appreciate her big, rowdy family even more.

She heard Riley dumping the broken glass into a trash bin. "Don't be a baby, Jack."

Hannah winced.

"What's with the bandage on your girlfriend's face?" Jack asked after a few seconds of silence. Hannah finished tying her shoe and padded down the hall to the kitchen.

"Car accident," Riley answered. "She knocked her head a bit, but she's going to be fine."

"I thought she was gonna cut me." Jack's voice was tinted with a smile. "I bet she'd be tough in a bar fight."

"I don't get into bar fights," Hannah said from the doorway.

Riley turned to look at her. She gazed back, not hiding her irritation. He shouldn't have sprung this crazy girlfriend cover story on her without warning her. And he shouldn't have been so harsh with his brother-in-law, who was clearly hurting from the loss of his sister just as much as Riley was hurting from the loss of his wife.

She looked away from Riley and smiled at Jack. "Have you had breakfast? I could probably make an omelet or something."

"I grabbed something at the diner in town," Jack answered, returning the smile. "Riley told me about your accident. I hope you're feeling better."

"We were up most of the night at the hospital," Riley answered quickly. "The doctors said she had a mild concussion, but they cut her loose this morning."

"Wow, I bet you're beat, then. Look, I can go find a place in town or something—"

"I started a fire in the wood stove," Hannah said quickly, darting a glance at Riley. He started this mess, so now he'd have to live with it. "The bed's made. I put a few of my things in there because Riley's closet is full, but there's plenty of space for you to put your things."

The look of alarm in Riley's eyes made her smile. *How's that surprise thing working for you now, big guy?*

"Are you sure?" Jack directed the question more toward Riley than Hannah.

He hesitated only a moment, genuine affection in his eyes. "Of course I'm sure," he said. "You're family."

Jack's grin made Hannah's stomach twist into a knot. The poor guy looked like a grateful puppy, happy he didn't get kicked out of the house once the new kid came along. "Can I do something around here?" he asked Riley, pushing to his feet. "I bet you two were too tired to check on the horses this morning—want me to go let 'em out into the pasture?"

"Would you? That would be great." Riley latched on to the idea quickly, no doubt wanting to get Jack out of the way so he and Hannah could finally get their stories straight.

"I'll be back in a bit." Jack winked in Hannah's direction, grabbed his hat from where he'd laid it on the counter by the door, and headed out the back, the screen door slamming behind him.

The ensuing silence made Hannah's skin prickle. Riley turned slowly to look at her. "Go on, say it."

"Your girlfriend?"

"What else was I supposed to say? He walks in on you in your robe, me in a towel—"

Her gaze fell on the towel, which had slipped down his

body a notch to reveal the hard, flat plane of his lower belly. She swallowed hard and forced her gaze back up to his face.

"We can't tell people why you're really here," he said.

She sighed. "How long do you think he'll be here?"

"I don't know. This is the first time he's been here since Emily died." He started to sit, until he apparently realized that he was wearing only a towel. He nodded toward the hallway, as if asking her to follow.

After a quick detour to the guest room to grab a few things she'd need, they went down the hall to Riley's bedroom. She waited outside, standing with her back against the wall while he entered his bedroom to dress. "I guess we should get our stories straight. But I should warn you, I'm not a good liar."

"So we keep it simple and as close to the truth as possible. Why did you come to Wyoming in the first place?" His voice was a bit muffled.

Trying hard not to picture a T-shirt sliding over his lean, muscular chest, she swallowed the lump in her throat. "Some friends invited me up to fish on their private lake, and then I planned to do the tourist thing at Grand Teton and Yellowstone."

Her friends, David and Julie Sexton, had a small ranch with a very good trout lake nestled in a valley in the Wind River Mountains. She'd spent the first four days of her vacation with them and their two school-age daughters.

If only she'd stayed there instead of deciding to do the typical tourist thing and visit the national parks—

"So we stick with that. You came here to go fishing, and we met by accident—"

She heard the sound of a zipper. Squeezing her eyes shut, she sighed. "And immediately started shacking up? I'm not that kind of girl."

"Hey, you're the one who gave Jack your room."

She glared at the opposite wall. "You started it with the girl-friend thing."

"Enough. Clearly, since you're not that kind of girl and I'm not really that kind of guy, we met months ago." He emerged from the bedroom dressed in jeans and a fresh T-shirt. "Maybe we met online."

If she'd thought a fully dressed Riley Patterson would be less distracting than a naked one, she'd been gravely mistaken. The T-shirt only emphasized the broadness of his shoulders and the powerful muscles of his chest, and the well-worn jeans fit him like a second skin.

Stop looking, Hannah. Looking leads to touching and touching leads to getting your heart shattered in a million pieces the day before your wedding—

She cleared her throat. "Where online?"

"I don't know. I don't go online much." Frustration lining his lean features, he headed toward the kitchen.

She followed. "Do you fish?" she asked.

He turned to look at her, leaning against the sink counter. "What is with the fishing thing?"

"My family runs a marina and fishing camp. I'm a fishing guide, among other things." She shot him a wry smile. "You're looking at the Crappie Queen of Gossamer Lake."

His lips quirked. "Okay, we met on a fishing Web site."

"Which one?"

He reached for the coffeemaker. "You tell me. You're the Crappie Queen."

Over coffee, they quickly outlined their cover story. They'd met online on Freshwater Expeditions, a fishing forum that put avid freshwater fishermen together with fishing guides all over the country. Hitting it off immediately, they'd formed a friendship that became something more, and Hannah had combined her planned fishing trip to Wyoming with the chance to finally meet Riley face-to-face.

"One thing led to another, and…"

"And now we're sleeping together." Hannah's forehead wrinkled as she finally realized the full implications of offering the guest room to Jack. She pushed away her unfinished cup of coffee and rubbed her tired eyes. "Mama's right. My temper always gets me in trouble."

"I've got a sleeping roll I can put on the floor."

She shook her head. "It's your bed. I'll take the roll."

"I've slept outdoors on the hard, cold ground before, plenty of times. Snugged up next to the wood stove will be a luxury." He carried their cups to the sink. "So we're set? Is our cover story close enough to the truth for you to handle?"

"I think so. But we should make a pact—we share whatever we tell Jack separately. There's a lot of room to mess up."

The rattle of the back door cut off any response he might have made. He grabbed his gun from the counter.

Jack entered the kitchen, his dark hair windblown and his cheeks bright with exercise. Riley relaxed, tucking the gun in the waistband of his jeans.

Jack's earlier glum mood was gone, replaced by a mischievous light in his dark eyes. "I took Jazz out for a run. He cut loose—you haven't been riding him much recently?"

"Not as much as I should," Riley admitted.

Hannah almost asked how many horses he had, then wondered if that was something they'd have discussed online. She slanted a quick look at Riley and found him looking a bit unnerved.

"Do you ride?" Jack asked Hannah.

"Yeah, though not as much as I'd like. In fact, we've been

thinking of buying some horses and offering trail rides in the spring and fall up Gossamer Mountain."

"Gossamer Mountain?"

"It's in Alabama," Riley interjected. "Hannah's family has a fishing camp up there. That's how we met."

"You met at a fishing camp in Alabama?" Jack looked at Riley with a confused expression. "When did you go to Alabama?"

"No, we met online. On a fishing forum," Riley said.

"You go online?" Jack's eyes widened further.

"Not a lot," Riley said defensively, as if his brother-in-law had accused him of being a nerd.

Hannah stifled a grin. "It's a forum called Freshwater Expeditions." She checked out the forum from time to time herself to keep up with what avid anglers were talking about. It was good for business. "We hit it off right away."

"And when Hannah made plans to visit some friends here in Wyoming, we decided to finally meet in person."

"And here we are." Hannah hoped her smile didn't look as brittle as it felt. Playacting wasn't one of her talents. It was nerve-racking, wondering if Jack Drummond was buying the load of bull she and Riley were selling.

Not to mention the way her rattled brain kept returning to the realization that she and Riley Patterson would be sharing a bedroom come nightfall.

"She seems nice."

Riley looked up from the case folder he was reading to find his brother-in-law's dark-eyed gaze on him. He set the folder on the coffee table. "I know this has been a kick in the teeth for you, Jack. I'm sorry we sprang it on you like that."

Jack pushed the rocking chair closer and propped his socked feet up on the coffee table. "Three years is a long time to be alone. I get that."

Pain settled over Riley, down to the bone. "I haven't stopped loving Em. I never will."

"But we both know she wouldn't want you to live the rest of your life alone," Jack said solemnly.

Lying to Jack about his fake relationship with Hannah was worse than Riley had anticipated. Each fib felt like a bitter betrayal of Emily and the love they'd shared. His skin prickled, as if the truth was trying to seep through his pores and shout itself to the world.

He wasn't over Emily! He hadn't moved on.

He never would.

"You look a little beat, Riley. You were up all night with Hannah at the hospital, weren't you?"

"Yeah," he answered, relieved to finally say something that was true. "It was an eventful night."

"Where'd she have her wreck?"

"Just outside of Whitmore—on the road toward Jackson."

"Isn't that way past here?"

Hell. "Yeah. She wanted to drive into Jackson to do some shopping." Women liked to shop, right? Emily always had.

"How'd the wreck happen?"

Riley tamped down his irritation. Jack's question wasn't unreasonable, and if he and Hannah weren't lying through their teeth, it wouldn't even matter. "Nobody's quite sure—Hannah doesn't remember much of what happened around the time of the wreck. The police think she might have been run off the road."

"Hit and run?"

"Something like that."

Jack cocked his head. "I'm surprised you're not out there hunting down the jerk who did it."

"There aren't any leads. And I'm more interested in taking care of Hannah." That was true, at least. His voice rang with conviction.

Jack smiled, although Riley still detected a hint of sadness in his eyes. "I like her, I think. I mean, what I've seen of her. She seems very down to earth. Emily would approve."

Pain sliced through Riley's chest at Jack's words. He took a couple of shallow breaths and looked away.

"I'm sorry if the way I acted this morning made you feel bad or anything." Jack leaned forward, laying his hand on Riley's arm. "You were a good husband to Emily. You deserve to be happy again."

Riley managed a smile, but inside, an ache had settled in the center of his chest. He pushed to his feet. "I'm going to check on Hannah. Make yourself at home."

Jack responded with a silent nod, his expression bemused.

Riley headed down the hallway to his bedroom, opening the door quietly. Hannah lay curled on her side beneath a plaid woolen blanket, her back to him. Walking softly so as not to wake her, he settled into the armchair by the window and watched her sleep. Early-afternoon light filtered through the curtains, bathing her face with shimmering rose color. She looked weary and battered, her face a roadmap of scrapes and bruises. But beneath the imperfections was beauty that even his shuttered soul couldn't miss.

He wondered if Jack was right. Would Emily have liked Hannah Cooper? If this charade were the truth instead of a necessary lie, would Emily approve?

He wasn't sure he wanted to know the answer.

THE AFTERNOON HAD WANED while she slept, cool blue shadows of twilight encroaching on the bedroom where she lay. She heard the sound of footfalls, boots on the hardwood floor. Riley, perhaps, coming to wake her for dinner.

She was warm and comfortable. She didn't want to move. Perhaps if she pretended she was still asleep—

As she started to close her eyes, something shimmered in the low light. She made out a curve of silver, complex shapes and shadows.

A silver belt buckle.

The breath left her lungs in a shaking hiss. She tried to stir, to escape the cottony cage of twilight slumber, but she was paralyzed. The bootfalls came closer, and she heard him breathing. Slow, steady and deadly.

Riley, she thought. *Where is Riley?*

She opened her mouth and tried to scream. Only a hoarse croak emerged. Her vision narrowed to the silver belt buckle moving inexorably closer.

A hand caught hers, tugging her up. She tried to fight, her movements sluggish and flailing.

"Hannah!" Riley's voice tore through the fabric of her nightmare, dragging her into consciousness with shocking speed. Her whole body buzzed with adrenaline, making her tremble.

Riley's hands cradled her face, his gaze intent. "Are you okay? You were crying out."

She dropped her head against his shoulder, pressing her nose into the curve of his neck. She breathed deeply, filling her lungs with his tangy scent. "I'm okay," she said, her voice muffled against the collar of his T-shirt.

He brushed her hair off her cheek. "Nightmare?"

She nodded, hoping he wouldn't pull away. It wouldn't hurt to cling a moment, would it? At least until the shivers eased.

He edged over, sliding onto the bed beside her. Tucking her against him, he waited patiently for her to relax. The silence between them was comfortable, she found to her surprise. She had not thought of him as someone who could provide much comfort, no matter how good his intentions.

"I'm okay," she repeated a little while later, afraid she'd tested his patience too long. She sat away from him, brushing her hair back from her damp face.

"Do you remember what you dreamed?"

She didn't really. Only the nagging sense that she'd seen something important lingered with her.

"You cried out as if you were afraid."

"I was," she admitted. "I just don't know why."

She couldn't tell if he was disappointed or not. He was good at hiding his feelings. He had turned on the lamp by the bed, casting a warm glow on the shadowy room. She must have slept most of the day, for outside the window the sky was dark and the room had grown uncomfortably chilly.

Riley crossed to the wood stove in the corner and added wood and kindling. The dying embers flickered to life.

When he turned back to her, the wary look in his eyes drove away the memory of their earlier ease. Though she couldn't read his thoughts in his shuttered expression, there was no softness there, only a tense watchfulness that made her skin prickle.

He sat beside her on the edge of the bed, his gaze searching hers, as if he wasn't sure she was telling the truth about not being able to remember. The silence between them became anything but comfortable, the air in the small bedroom crackling with electric awareness.

Looking away, she swallowed hard and tried to remember

whatever it was that was hovering just on the outer edges of her memory. There had been fear. Darkness.

A glimmer of metal, curves and recesses...

"A snake," she said, her voice faint.

"A snake?"

She looked up and met his quizzical gaze. "The man who attacked me. I remembered what was on his silver belt buckle. It was a rattlesnake."

Chapter Six

"She thinks it's in the shape of a rattlesnake, or some sort of snake." Riley spoke softly into his cell phone, intensely aware of his brother-in-law moving around in the guest bedroom just down the hall.

"That's not exactly a unique design," Joe warned.

"It's more than we had," Riley said. "Can we put someone on it, get some pictures for Hannah to choose from?"

"Needle in a haystack," Joe said tightly.

"More than we had," Riley repeated.

"I'll put Jane on it. She's been wanting to do something besides sit home waiting for the baby to come, and it's safer than the patrol job she's been trying to talk me into."

"Thanks."

"How's it going now that Jack's in town?"

"A little harder than I'd planned. But so far, so good."

Of course, he still had a long night alone with Hannah in his bedroom to look forward to.

Hearing the sound of footsteps coming down the hallway, he rang off with Joe and turned to find Hannah standing in the kitchen doorway, her dark hair tousled and her eyes soft with sleepiness. Though her gray sweats hid her tempting curves, she still fired his blood in a way no woman had since Emily's death.

What the hell was going on with him? Why her, why now? He couldn't have chosen a worse situation—or woman— to rediscover that he was still a living, breathing, healthy male.

She hovered in the doorway. "I could fix something for dinner," she suggested, her raspy voice sending a shiver of pleasure skating down his back. "I mean, I'm not a great cook or anything, but I'm pretty good with a can opener."

Her wry smile made her green eyes sparkle, and Riley had to look away.

"You're still recuperating." His voice came out gruff.

"I'm not sick." She sounded defensive in response.

He looked up, annoyed with himself and the way this whole situation was spiraling out of control. But before he had a chance to apologize, Jack walked up behind Hannah and put his hands on her shoulders.

She gave a start, but Jack calmed her quickly with a gentle squeeze. "How about I handle dinner?" he suggested, guiding her into the kitchen. "I've been dying to try out a chili recipe I got from a saucy little *señorita* I met down in Laredo." He winked at Hannah, grinning broadly.

Riley squelched an unwelcome rush of irritation at his brother-in-law's easy familiarity with Hannah. "I don't know if you'll be able to find chili fixings here. I haven't done a lot of grocery shopping recently."

"I drove to town while you two were resting." Jack arched an eyebrow at Riley, grinning when Riley scowled in response. He crossed to the cabinet and pulled out a large canvas bag full of his purchases. "You know, that little place on Canyon Road has a really good fresh-produce stand. I had to pay a pretty penny, but it'll be worth it." He turned to Hannah. "How are you with a chopping knife, gorgeous?"

Hannah smiled, clearly pleased to have something to do besides lie in bed. She took the knife Jack handed her and went to work chopping onions and peppers.

Riley watched her deft hands make short work of the vegetables. "You're good with a knife."

She looked up with a start, her knife slipping and nicking her knuckle. "Damn it!" She sucked her knuckle between her lips, her forehead wrinkling.

"I'm sorry—" He grabbed a couple of paper towels from the dispenser and ran them under the tap. Taking her hand, he dabbed at the blood to check how badly she'd cut herself.

"It's nothing," she said. But she didn't pull her hand away as he applied a little pressure to the shallow nick.

"I'll get a bandage." Jack set aside the beef tips he was seasoning and headed toward the bathroom.

"I told you I wasn't much of a cook," she said, her cheeks flushed and her lips curved with a rueful smile.

"I startled you." They stood so close he could smell the apple soap she'd used when she'd showered earlier. The scent reminded him of spring—fresh, crisp and full of promise.

Her green eyes darkened. "I guess I'm still jumpy."

His blood simmered, slow and hot in his veins. He'd forgotten the feel of fire licking low in his belly and pulsing hunger drumming in his chest.

"Here we go." Jack returned to the kitchen with the first-aid kit Riley kept in the bathroom. He eased Riley aside and pulled out a tube of antibiotic ointment.

As Jack bandaged Hannah's hand, Riley crossed to the back door and pushed aside the faded curtain, looking out into the deepening blue of nightfall. A chill wind rolled down the mountains, rattling the door. He was tempted to step outside, into the bitter breeze, and let it cool his burning thoughts.

How was he going to make it through a night alone with Hannah Cooper without losing his mind?

Once bandaged, Hannah finished her task of chopping vegetables. She and Jack worked together with enviable ease preparing the chili, while Riley kept a watchful distance. With Jack, Hannah laughed, she joked, she sparkled like a jewel set incongruously in the middle of his plain, utilitarian kitchen.

This was the real Hannah Cooper, Riley realized. The one unencumbered by fear. The woman she must have been when she arrived in Wyoming, before a killer had tried to make her his next victim. She didn't have to think about clues or harsh memories with Jack. She could just be Hannah, the woman from Alabama who'd come to Wyoming to go fishing and see Old Faithful and the Grand Teton mountains.

Jack was right, Riley realized with some pain. Emily would have loved Hannah.

Despite her long nap that afternoon, Hannah didn't make it through dinner without breaking into yawns.

"We're boring her already," Jack teased.

She gave a rueful laugh. "I promise I can stay awake long enough to help with the dishes."

"No, you don't." Riley broke his silence. "You go on and get to bed. Jack and I can handle a few dishes."

She gave him an odd look, then pushed herself out of her chair and offered them both a soft good-night.

After she'd gone down the hall, Jack looked at Riley. "You were quiet during dinner."

"I figured you and Hannah had conversation covered," he replied drily, immediately kicking himself for the irritation in his tone. He was acting like a jealous jerk.

Ironically, it worked in his favor. "I'm not moving in on your girl, Riley. I know I've got a reputation as a player, but you're family. I wouldn't do that to you."

Riley made himself laugh, although inside his guts were in a tangle. "I know."

"And you know, you guys don't have to be all proper and formal around me. It's not going to kill me to see you kiss the girl." Shooting Riley a pointed look, Jack got up and started putting away the leftover chili.

The image Jack's words evoked made Riley's mouth grow dry. What would it feel like to kiss her? To feel her soft curves settle against his body as if she'd been made exactly for him? The need to know was suddenly overwhelming.

He had to get out of the house. Now. Go take a ride, work off some of the restless energy tormenting him. But before he could act on the impulse, there was a knock at the back door.

Riley made sure his Ruger was tucked firmly in his waistband, ignoring Jack's curious look. He crossed to the back door and edged the faded curtains away from the inset window.

Joe and Jane Garrison stood outside, stamping from foot to foot against the cold night air.

Riley unlocked the door and let them inside, giving Joe a warning glance. He'd already told his friend about Jack's unexpected arrival and the charade he and Hannah had to keep up in front of his brother-in-law.

Joe and Jack knew each other from way back, but Jane hadn't yet met his brother-in-law. Joe handled the introductions, and Jane immediately engaged Jack in conversation, giving Joe a chance to show Riley the file he'd brought over.

"Jane spent the last couple of hours online, tracking down all the snake-shaped belt buckles she could find. She printed them out and they're all in here. I thought you'd want to see them as soon as possible, while the dream is still fresh in Hannah's mind." Joe handed over the folder. "Also, I've asked Jim Tanner to fax me the personnel files of the hospital security staff as soon as he gets access to them. His people will run the background checks, but I figure it won't hurt to put both departments to work on it."

"Good idea," Riley agreed. "If you do get them, I'll bring Hannah to the office. Give her a chance to get out and take in a little fresh air." Maybe, with people around, he wouldn't find himself thinking about the softness of her skin or wondering what she tasted like.

Because if he didn't get control of his treacherous body soon, the next four days would be the longest of his life.

A WAXING MOON HUNG LOW in the eastern sky, spreading cool blue light across the mountain in the distance. Beyond, the night was alive with stars, millions of them, more visible than Hannah could ever remember. She had grown up in one of the more remote areas of Alabama, where there weren't enough city lights to obscure the stars in the night sky, but even at home, she had never seen quite so many stars as this.

She couldn't orient herself, an odd feeling. She knew the window of Riley's darkened bedroom faced east, or she couldn't have seen the moon from this vantage point. But what was east when you didn't know where you were in the first place?

She had always prided herself on being aware of her surroundings, of picking up on the nuances of her settings that most people never even noticed. She was as skilled a tracker as any of her brothers, as good a boatman, as successful a fisherman and she was the best night hiker in the family.

She didn't like feeling so up-ended. It reminded her too

much of that moment, four years ago, when she watched her future shatter into a million pieces.

She leaned her forehead against the cool windowpane, feeling the vibration of the night wind rattling the glass. In a little while, Riley Patterson would walk through the bedroom door behind her and they'd close themselves into this small, intimate room for the night. The thought gave her a sense of safety, the knowledge that in this place, with Riley watching over her, nothing outside could hurt her.

But with that sense of safety came another, more complicated feeling of reckless anticipation. Riley would be there soon, so close she could hear him breathing, and she could hardly wait.

It was crazy. He was still clearly mourning a wife he'd never stop loving, and their acquaintance was supposed to be businesslike and short, spanning no more than the next few days. She'd been around other attractive men before without feeling like a schoolgirl trembling with a crush. Far more suitable and available men.

Or was that the appeal? Her brothers always teased her about her competitive streak. Did she think she had a fighting chance at winning his heart away from the other woman this time?

Go for it, Hannah. Maybe you've got a better shot against a dead woman.

Idiot.

She pushed her hair back from her face, wincing as her palm brushed against the scrape on her forehead. She had to get control over herself before she did something stupid.

A soft knock on the door behind her made her nerves twitch. The door swung open, spilling light from the hallway into the darkened bedroom. Hannah turned to look at Riley as he entered, her heart suddenly hammering against her breastbone.

He paused in the doorway a moment, a tall, lean silhouette against the light. She couldn't see his eyes in his shadowy face, but she felt his gaze like a touch. She felt suddenly naked, despite the warm flannel enveloping her from chin to ankle.

He reached for the light switch.

"Don't," she said. She wasn't ready to come into the harsh light of reality yet.

He hesitated a moment, then dropped his hand to his side and closed the door behind them, plunging the bedroom into darkness again.

Hannah turned back to the window, leaning her hot cheek against the cold glass pane. "You can see the mountain better without the light on."

Warmth washed over her as Riley edged close to the window, just behind her. Though he didn't touch her, she felt him as surely as if he had. "That's Sawyer's Rise."

"The mountain?"

"Yes." He moved the curtain aside, stepping up beside her. She looked up and found moonlight painting his masculine features a cool, shadowy-blue, emphasizing the hard, lean lines of his cheekbones and the deep cleft of his chin.

In this light, he looked as if he'd been carved from the face of the mountain, solid rock with a million unexpected facets. The itch to touch him tingled in her fingertips. Would he feel like stone, cool and rough to the touch?

After a moment of exquisite tension, he spoke again. "There's something I need to show you."

He moved away from the window. A moment later, the soft glow of lamplight filled the bedroom, obscuring the moonlit landscape outside behind the reflected light in the window-pane. Hannah caught a glimpse of herself in the reflection, her hair a tousled mess, her cheeks flushed beneath shadowy eyes.

She turned away quickly, running a hand through her hair to tame the riotous tumble. "What is it?"

He was carrying a thin manila folder, she saw. He sat on the bed and opened it, patting the mattress beside him.

She took a seat where he indicated and looked at what lay inside the folder. There were photos, obviously pulled from the Internet and printed on a color printer. Belt buckles, in a variety of snake shapes.

"Jane was a busy woman this evening," he murmured. "Do any of these look familiar?"

Hannah took the folder from him and started leafing through the printouts. None of the belt buckles jumped out at her. So much about the attack on her that day remained fuzzy, whether from the aftereffects of her concussion or the sheer trauma of the ambush. The more she tried to force herself to remember, the more confused the effort seemed to leave her. "I'm not sure," she said honestly.

"Can you eliminate any of them?"

She looked again. There were a couple of designs where the snake itself was the belt buckle. She was sure that hadn't been the case with her assailant. "Not these," she said, setting those pictures aside. "And not these two, either," she added, culling out a couple that were a dark, weathered pewter rather than a soft, shiny silver.

"That helps," he said, although she heard a faint strain of frustration in his voice.

She stood up and began laying the other printouts on the bed, placing them in a grid. When she was finished, she stepped back and closed her eyes, trying to clear her mind so she could go back to the day of the attack.

She'd been driving down the highway, hoping to make Jackson before nightfall. But she hadn't been speeding—

she'd checked her speedometer when she saw the blue light behind her.

"I pulled over," she said aloud. "I reached for my purse and got my driver's license. I turned back to the window, and I saw only his midsection. He had jeans on, and he was wearing a silver belt buckle—" The image in her mind came into sharp focus suddenly. It was oval-shaped, fashioned of silver with black detailing. The snake was coiled, its diamond-shaped head in the center of the buckle as if ready to strike.

She opened her eyes and looked at Riley. He was looking at the images, a deep furrow in his brow.

She looked down at the images, scanning them to see if any matched the belt buckle she remembered. She spotted it, third from the left, middle row. As she reached for it, Riley moved forward at the same time. Their hands met over the image.

Electric tingles rippled up her arm. She looked up, surprised, to find him staring at her, a strange intensity shining in his blue eyes.

"Is that the one?" His fingers tightened over hers.

She nodded, suddenly breathless.

A triumphant grin spread slowly over his face.

"How did you know?" she asked, looking down at his hand still covering hers on top of the color print.

He let go of her hand and stood, crossing to the desk near the window. He pulled a thick file folder from the bottom drawer and brought it over to the bed. "Can you put away all of the other prints?" he asked, already thumbing through the file in his lap.

She replaced all the useless printouts in the manila folder from which they'd come and held on to the one she'd identified, looking at it more closely. It was definitely the one she'd seen that day. But if it was a popular style—

"Here." Riley held out a piece of paper.

She took it from him, wincing as she realized it was an autopsy photo. The photo showed a close-up image of a woman's abdomen, from the bottom of the breasts to the pelvic bone. A dark bruise marred the skin of the upper belly, just below the ribcage.

Riley pointed to the bruise. "Can you see that?"

She looked closer. Suddenly, the bruise started to take a recognizable shape. "Oh, my God. It's the belt buckle."

She looked up at him, surprised to find him laughing softly. He dropped the file folder on the bed and reached for her hand, pulling her up and into his arms. His laughter vibrating against her chest, he swirled her around and around until her head swam.

He set her down, finally, still laughing softly as he kept her close. "You don't know how long I've been puzzling over that bruise," he murmured against her hair, his grip tightening.

Tentatively, she moved her hands up his sides, tracing the whipcord muscles lining his ribcage. Deep in her belly, heat pooled, setting off tiny tremors that rippled up her spine. Her breathing sped up as her heart began to pound like a hammer against her ribcage.

Oh, God, it was happening again.

Riley pulled back slowly, his gaze meeting hers. His eyes went midnight dark, and she realized he'd felt the traitorous response of her body to his. His eyes darkened, but not with anger or surprise. Where her hand rested against his chest, she felt the racing of his heart. Resistance fell away, leaving only hard, ravening need.

Kiss me, she thought, her breath trapped in her aching lungs.

She nearly collapsed to the floor when he let her go.

Chapter Seven

Riley crossed to the window and gazed out, as if he could see the mountains instead of his own traitorous reflection there. His whole body was humming with awareness. He could even hear Hannah's soft, quick respirations behind him.

"This is a break in the case, isn't it?" she asked.

He took a deep, steadying breath. He could control himself, damn it. He'd become very good at self-discipline over the last few years.

He turned to look at her. "Her name was Cara Sandifer. A rancher found her body in an irrigation pond a few hours after she was killed." He crossed to the bed, keeping his distance from her, and added the printout of the belt buckle to Cara's file. "Because her body was found so quickly, the evidence in her case is probably the best we have at the moment."

"We should tell someone. Joe. You should call Joe."

Riley nodded. "He can fax a notice over to other law-enforcement agencies in the area. We'll also track down the manufacturer and see how many belt buckles we're looking at, what stores in Wyoming carry them, that kind of thing."

He glanced at Hannah and found her sitting in the middle of the bed, her knees tucked up against her body protectively, the same way she'd sat in the hospital watching the crime-scene investigators go over her bed. Compassion trumped his uneasiness, and he crossed to her side, reaching out to squeeze her arm. "This is good news. You really came through for us."

She lifted her chin, unfolding out of her self-protective tuck until she sat cross-legged. When she spoke, her voice was stronger. "I hope it helps you find him. That's all I want, you know. To find this guy and go back home in one piece."

Her tone didn't change, but Riley couldn't miss the warning in her words. She may have felt the same charge of electricity between them that he'd experienced, but she was no more interested in pursuing it than he was.

That should make things between them considerably less complicated, he thought with relief.

He should have known better.

"THERE ARE 450 STORES in 36 states that carry the Cal Reno brand buckles. Most of those have, at one time or another, carried the Rattler design. At least thirty of those stores are located in Wyoming, and God knows how many there are in the surrounding states." Joe Garrison's expression was grim.

Hannah stared at the police chief, her heart sinking. "That many?"

"We've put out a request to track the purchases, but if someone made the purchase with cash, there's really no way to identify him. We can hope he paid with a credit card." Joe looked apologetic.

"Well, maybe we'll get lucky," Hannah said, not ready to let go of optimism. She glanced at Riley. His expression was shuttered, but she was beginning to figure out how to read him. It was all in his eyes. He couldn't hide his feelings in those expressive blue eyes.

Right now, he was feeling wary. Afraid to hope but, like her, not ready to give up yet. She felt an odd sense of camaraderie with him, as if the two of them were pitted against the rest of the doubting world.

Unfortunately, camaraderie with Riley Patterson wasn't really what she wanted to feel. If last night's restless attempt at slumber had proved anything, it was that all her good intentions, and all the hard lessons of her past, made poor preventatives against her attraction to the man.

Just the sound of his slow, steady breathing had been enough to fire her fantasies, and she'd tossed and turned all night, trying to fight their potent allure.

He wasn't even that good-looking, she had tried to tell herself, even as her skin still remembered the feel of his body pressed so tightly against hers. His craggy features were too rough-hewn to be considered conventionally handsome, his rusty hair close-cropped, almost military style, and worthless for running one's fingers through.

Except she kept finding herself imagining the crisp texture of his hair sliding beneath her fingertips, and the mere thought made her whole body tingle with anticipation.

An image of Craig's face flashed through her mind. So handsome, so familiar. She hadn't been able to keep her hands off him, either.

And hadn't that worked out well?

"What about the personnel files from the hospital?" Riley asked Joe.

"Jim called this morning. He was having a little trouble working out the legal details, but he found a judge late last night who'd sign the court order for access to the records. Only he can't share them outside his jurisdiction, so we'll have to wait for his people to work through the list," Joe said.

"That could take forever," Riley protested, running his left hand over his jaw, clearly frustrated.

Morning sunlight slicing into the room between the kitchen window curtains reflected off the slim gold band on his ring finger, catching Hannah's attention. She let her gaze linger on the ring as it provided a much-needed reality check.

Riley Patterson might be sexy. He might be the kind of rugged, masculine man that made ordinarily sane women consider moving to Wyoming and roughing it through long, harsh winters just to sleep at night in such a man's arms.

But in the ways that mattered most, Riley Patterson was a married man. His love for his wife drove him, day in and day out, to find an elusive killer who'd left few clues to follow. His body might respond like a man when he was around a woman, just as he'd responded to being close to her last night. But his heart was strictly off-limits.

"I know it's frustrating that we can't get all the answers immediately," Joe said, giving Hannah something to think about besides her alarming attraction to Riley. "But this is pretty significant movement on these cases. That's good news."

Riley nodded. "I know you're right. It's just—" He looked at Hannah.

"So maybe you should spend your time trying to concentrate on what else Hannah can remember," Joe suggested.

Footsteps on the back porch heralded Jack Drummond's return from the stable. Joe stuffed the files he'd been sharing with them in his briefcase and rose from the table as Jack walked into the kitchen. "Hi there, Jack."

Jack shook hands with Joe. "Back so soon?"

As Joe responded, and their greeting turned into small talk, Riley leaned toward Hannah, his voice lowered. "I think Joe's right. We need to concentrate on helping you remember more of what happened the day of the attack."

"Every time I try to concentrate on it, I just become more confused," she said softly. "I don't even know what would help at this point."

"I have some thoughts—"

Jack cleared his throat loudly. "Can't even leave these lovebirds alone for five seconds before they've got their heads together, whispering sweet nothings, Joe. What am I gonna do with them?"

"Short of hosing them down?" Joe responded, shooting a wink at Hannah.

"Well, they'll have themselves a little free time today, because I'm heading into town to see if I can stir up a little trouble." Jack held his hands up toward Joe. "Strictly legal, of course."

"Of course." Joe patted Jack on the back and turned to Riley. "I'll let you know if I hear anything about that case I was telling you about. Enjoy your time off."

"Thanks." Riley walked Joe out, while Jack settled into the chair his brother-in-law had vacated.

"You could ditch Riley and come to town with me, you know," Jack said with a wicked grin. "I'd show you places in Canyon Creek Riley probably doesn't even know about—"

"I heard that," Riley shot over his shoulder as he closed the door behind Joe. "And you'd be surprised the places I know about in Canyon Creek, son." He crossed to Jack's side and clamped his hands on his brother-in-law's shoulders. "Like where to bury a body so nobody can find it."

"Okay, okay, I'm going!" Jack said, laughing. He headed down the hall toward his room.

"He's right about one thing," Riley said, holding out his hand to Hannah. "Let's get out of this house."

THE MORNING WAS TURNING out to be unseasonably mild for October in Wyoming, the bright, late-morning sun warming the cab of Riley's pickup truck. Hannah laid her head back against the headrest and closed her eyes, enjoying the light on her face and the slow, bluesy strains of a Tim McGraw song playing on the truck's radio.

If it weren't for Riley's steady stream of questions, she might even be able to pretend it was a carefree outing.

"What had you been doing before you headed west on 287?"

She opened her eyes, releasing a soft sigh. "I'd spent longer on the lake at my friends' place than I'd intended. The trout were biting great, so we decided to eat some of our catch for lunch. I'd planned to be on the road before lunch, but I couldn't pass up the fresh fish, so I didn't get out of there as early as I'd hoped."

"You were about twenty miles southwest of Grand Teton State Park when you were pulled over, right?"

"That's what Sheriff Tanner said. I don't know for sure."

Riley's brow creased. "Would you be able to recognize where you were pulled over if you saw it again?"

"I don't know. Maybe. I know it was fairly isolated, and there was no shoulder of the road to speak of. I pulled over just past a crossroad, because there was finally a little bit of a rocky shoulder to pull over on." She turned to look at him, wincing a little as her seatbelt pressed against her still-sore body. "Would it help to find the place?"

"I suppose the Teton County Sheriff's Department has already looked for it, but—yeah. I think it would help. Maybe it would jog your memory, if nothing else."

"If we're lucky," she agreed, although the thought of re-creating the nightmare of that day held little appeal. Still, if it helped Riley get closer to stopping a killer, she'd do it.

"Where do your friends live?"

"It's a small ranch in the Pavillion area."

He nodded. "I know the area. Do you think you could find it again?"

"You want us to go there? Today?"

"I want us to start where you started, when you started. The more directly we duplicate your drive, the better." He reached into his pocket for his cell phone and dialed a number. "Hey, Joe, it's Riley."

As Riley outlined the plan over the phone with his boss, Hannah turned her gaze back toward the landscape unfolding ahead of them. They were driving east, toward Canyon Creek. The plan had originally been to stop for lunch in town, just to give Hannah a chance to get out of the house. The countryside outside of town was mostly ranch acreage, punctuated by scrub grass and the occasional small lake or winding creek. Horses and cattle dotted the grassy pastureland, although Riley had told her that the grazing season was mostly over for the year.

"Anything new from Jackson?" Riley asked. His lips pressed to a line as he listened to Joe's response. "Yeah, I know I just talked to you a half hour ago. Yeah. Bye."

"Still nothing?"

He shook his head. "Jackson has this stuff on rush, which is really all we could hope for, given we haven't definitively made the connection between your attack and the murders."

"But the belt buckle—"

"The state lab guys will look at what we sent them. But they have other cases."

Hannah slumped against her seat, frustrated. It was a lot easier to be patient with the snail's pace of forensic science when you weren't the one whose life had been upended, she supposed. And she knew the Wyoming authorities were probably working as quickly as they could.

"So, are we still going into town?" she asked aloud.

"Yeah. You left your friend's place in Pavillion when?"

"Around two in the afternoon."

"Good. We've got time to grab lunch and a car and still get to your starting point by two."

"A car?"

"You were driving a Pontiac G6. I can probably talk Lewis at the used-car place into letting us borrow something similar."

They reached town within ten minutes. Other than a distinctive western feel to the town's buildings, and the sprawling blue Wyoming sky spreading out for miles beyond the town's small cluster of business and in-town residences, Canyon Creek, Wyoming, was not that different from her own hometown of Gossamer Ridge, Alabama. The friendly waves from pedestrians and drivers alike as they drove down Main Street were something she encountered daily at home. Everybody knew everybody else in a small town.

Which meant, of course, that she attracted plenty of curious looks as people realized that Riley Patterson wasn't alone in his Chevy Silverado.

"Same story as we're telling Jack?" she asked aloud as he pulled into the parking lot of a small used-car lot.

He looked at her, his brow furrowed. "Same story?"

"People will want to know who I am."

His brow creased further. "Ah, damn. You're right."

"We can pretend I'm a cousin or something—"

"No, it's okay. Now that Jack knows you're here, it's not like he's going to keep quiet about it. People will probably be so thrilled to see me out with a woman, they'll bend over backwards to leave us be." There was a bitter edge to his voice that made Hannah's stomach hurt.

Yet she understood what he was feeling, more than he knew. "Everyone keeps waiting for my brother, J.D., to fall in love again," she said. "And it's been almost eight years for him."

He stopped with his hand on the door handle. "Eight years since what?"

"Since his wife was murdered."

THE WORKSHOP in his mother's root cellar was small but private, just as he required. She'd become too arthritic to handle the rough wooden stairs a few years before she died, making the cellar solely his domain for almost a decade now. Besides the house access, the cellar also had an outside entrance built into the ground. Its wide double doors accommodated easy loading and unloading from the Crown Vic parked in the side yard, and the extra insulation he'd added a few years back made the room virtually soundproof.

He sat on the work stool, polishing his tools and reviewing the last two days in his mind, determined to fix what had gone wrong not once but twice in the past forty-eight hours. There was no way to candy-coat the truth. The girl had caught him by surprise. She'd kept her head, despite the pepper-spray ambush, and managed to get away. She'd almost drawn blood, he thought, looking down at the light scrape on his pinky finger where the ring had been the day before.

Worse, she'd thwarted his careful plan to mop up his mess. He should've known she was awake. He should have heard her breath quicken, seen her furtive movements to undo the IV cannula. He'd gotten sloppy, and things were now worse than before. The cops were putting the pieces together, after all he'd done to spread out his kills in different jurisdictions and different years. He'd overheard the cops talking about the kills at the hospital. Three years of murders, they'd said.

He smiled with the first real satisfaction he'd felt in two days. Three years wasn't even close.

His first kill had been almost ten years ago. A neighbor girl, not a half mile down the highway. She'd been seventeen. He'd been twenty.

It had been sweet. So very sweet.

He laid down his knife and reached across the worktable for the folder that he'd compiled after his earlier visit to the Teton County Sheriff's Department. It had been so easy—stop by to see an old friend from his prison-guard days who'd made the move to real police work. He'd just kept his eyes open, grabbed the file when his friend wasn't looking and stuck the folder under his coat. So easy. A quick trip to the copy shop down the street and a return trip to the sheriff's station on pretense of leaving his cell phone behind, and he'd had everything he needed.

Nobody had suspected a thing. And now he had his own file on Hannah Jean Cooper of Gossamer Ridge, Alabama.

It didn't do much to tell him where she was at the moment, but quick phone calls to her home number and work number had, at least, given him hope that she had not yet left Wyoming. He still had time to tie up that loose end.

Meanwhile, he thought, turning to look at the woman lying gagged and bound on the worktable, he had work to do.

"Your brother's wife was murdered?" Riley's stomach muscles clenched.

She nodded, her expression grim. "Eight years ago next February. She was abducted from the trucking company where she worked—she'd worked late and her car battery had died, stranding her alone. By the time anyone realized she was missing, it was already too late."

"I'm sorry." The words seemed inadequate.

"My brother was devastated. In some ways, he still is." Moisture sparkled on her eyelashes. She sniffed back the tears. "So, you see, I know it's hard to deal with people who think you can just get over it and move on. I've watched my brother deal with it for years."

"Did the police ever find out who killed her?" As soon as he asked the question, Riley realized he didn't want to know the answer. Three years without answers had been a living horror. The idea of eight years of not knowing who'd upended his whole world was almost more than he could stand.

"J.D. hasn't stopped searching, either," Hannah said, her voice small and strangled.

"Then you understand," he said grimly.

She nodded, sniffing again. She took a deep breath, squared her jaw and turned to look at him. "You do whatever makes you comfortable. Tell people whatever you want. I'll go along with it."

He wished it were that simple. But Jack's arrival had complicated everything. Once Riley blurted the first thing that had come to his mind to explain Hannah's presence, the die had been cast. He'd have to go on with the charade.

"We could tell Jack the truth," Hannah said, as if reading his mind.

He shook his head. "No, we can't."

"Don't you trust him?"

He rubbed his jaw, wishing he could say yes without hesitation. "Jack's a good guy. He wouldn't hurt you or me on purpose for the world. But he's also the kind of guy who thinks Saturday nights are made for drinking himself under the table, and I know from experience that he can't keep his tongue when he's drinking."

Her brow furrowed. "I see."

"We have to go on with what we've started." He began to open the truck's driver-side door, but Hannah stayed him with a hand on his arm.

She tightened her grip on his forearm. "I'll wait here in the truck."

"That's only delaying the questions. It won't make them go away," he warned.

"I know. But look at it this way—when I'm finally out of here, you can just pretend things between us didn't work out, and then you'll get a reprieve while you get over our failed romance." She smiled at him, her eyes sparkling with amusement at figuring out a way to turn their uncomfortable charade into a plus.

Her humor was infectious. He felt his own lips starting to curve with a smile. "You're devious. I like that."

She laughed at that. "Six older brothers will do that for you."

He smiled again, surprised how much he enjoyed having someone to conspire with again. It had been one of the things he'd enjoyed most about his marriage to Emily—someone to keep secrets with, to cocoon himself with against the often cold and indifferent world outside.

But as he entered the used-car lot's office and answered the greetings of the staff, it occurred to him that getting comfortable around Hannah Cooper could turn out to be a very dangerous proposition.

Chapter Eight

"It's sort of like truth or dare without the dare part. Or strip poker, without the stripping." Hannah cut the deck of playing cards she'd talked Riley into picking up at the service station where they'd stopped for gas and a couple of deli sandwiches. "My brothers Jake and Gabe made it up. Come to think of it, there might have been a dare aspect to it early on, but I think Mom ended that after the tree-house incident."

He looked at her skeptically as he gathered up the remains of their lunch and set them aside to drop in the trash can later. "Why do you call it popsmack?"

She grinned. "I'm pretty sure it's because my brothers ended up in a huge punching match by the end of every game. They're cretins." She lightened the insult with affection; her brothers, for all the irritation they'd been over the years, were good guys, and she loved them all dearly.

"Couldn't we just play strip poker instead?" Riley flashed her a leering grin, but she saw the nervousness behind his eyes. He was clearly a private kind of guy, and what she was asking him to do had to be pretty daunting.

"It's just a getting to know you kind of thing," she assured him, dealing half the cards to him atop the weathered picnic table, dealing the other half to herself.

They'd arrived early in Pavillion, since they hadn't stopped to eat in town, so they had a couple of hours to pass before they could head toward Jackson to recreate the events leading up to the event. Talk had been sparse during the drive, Riley sinking into a sort of contemplative silence for most of the way. No doubt going over all the facts of the cases he was investigating. He was nothing if not single-minded.

But their discussion about Jack and his relative trustworthiness had convinced Hannah that she and Riley needed to get their stories straight if they were going to spend much more time in Jack's company. Riley's brother-in-law was good-natured and mostly benign, but he wasn't stupid. They had to be convincing as lovers, and that included knowing a little more about each other than just their names. She'd hoped popsmack would prove a fun way to make that happen.

"It's very simple—you play your cards one at a time. The person with the highest card wins."

"Which means?"

"Which means the winner gets to ask any question he or she wants, and the other person has to answer that question honestly."

The wary look in his eyes deepened. "What if it's a really personal question?"

"Jack thinks we're sleeping together. I think that means we should know a few really personal things about each other."

His shoulders squared and the muscles in his jaw twitched tight. "Okay, let's go."

She picked up her half of the deck and dealt the top card. A three of clubs.

Across the table, Riley smiled. When he dealt a ten of hearts, his smile widened. "So, I can ask you anything?"

Hannah's stomach tightened. He looked entirely too pleased with the idea. "Yeah, anything."

He thought for a minute. "What's your favorite color?"

"Blue," she answered quickly, torn between relief and disappointment. If they both got cold feet about asking the hard questions, this game would go nowhere.

She dealt another card. Queen of spades. He dealt a five of clubs and gave her a narrow-eyed look.

"What made you decide to be a policeman?" she asked.

His expression eased. "I didn't want to be a rancher, and Joe was my best friend. So when he decided to become a police officer, I thought it sounded like my kind of adventure."

"And was it?"

He quirked an eyebrow. "I don't remember follow-up questions being part of the game rules."

As he started to deal another card, she put her hand over his. "Seriously. Do you like being a cop?"

He looked down at her hand on his. She started to pull it away, but he reached out and trapped it with his other hand. "If we're supposed to be lovers, I think we should probably get used to touching each other."

Her heart turned an erratic little flip. He was right, of course, but her mind hadn't stopped with just holding hands. Would Jack expect to see them embrace? Even kiss?

"Should we be playing spin the bottle instead?" she muttered nervously.

His grip on her hand softened into something alarmingly like a caress. His thumb moved slowly over the back of her hand. "Probably."

He's still married in his heart, she reminded herself silently. *He still loves his wife.* She eased her hand from between his and reached for her deck.

"I do like being a cop," he said before she could deal her next card, his blue-eyed gaze direct. "I haven't been in a position to enjoy the investigative aspect of the job that much in a place like Canyon Creek, but I like being one of the go-to guys in town. People trust me to protect them. Make sure justice is done. I like being useful."

She smiled. "You sound like my brother, Aaron. He's a deputy sheriff back home."

"What about your older brother—the one who lost his wife?"

She toyed with the stack of cards in front of her. "He was in the Navy awhile—he worked in ship maintenance. When he left the service, he came back to the marina to help my parents run the place. They'd been wanting to offer on-site service to our slip renters, and now J.D. does that full-time. He likes tinkering with things, making them work."

Riley flipped the top card of his stack on to the table face up. "Five of spades."

She dealt a card. "Nine of diamonds."

He smiled slightly. "Your turn."

She was beginning to wish she'd never started this game. The more she learned about him, the more she liked, and she had a feeling he'd be a lot easier to resist if she didn't like him quite so much.

"What's your favorite food?" she asked finally.

His mouth quirked. "Lost your nerve?"

"It's better than 'what's your favorite color?'" she shot back with a roll of her eyes.

"Fair enough." He rubbed his chin as if giving her question some thought. "Would steak and potatoes be too much of a cliché?"

"Not if it's the truth."

He smiled. "I do like a good steak, but I guess my favorite food is barbecue ribs."

"My brother Jake makes the best ribs," she said, her mouth watering at the thought. "Slow cooked, slathered with his homemade sauce—yum. He cooked some for Labor Day."

"I make my own barbecue sauce, too," he said. "Actually, it's Emily's recipe—"

The air between them grew immediately colder. Riley sat back from the table, his fingers tapping the stack of undealt cards in front of him, moving them forward toward her.

"I wish I could have met her," Hannah said. She immediately regretted her words when she saw the flash of pain cross Riley's face.

"We should probably get on the road." He looked away.

She scooped up the cards and put them back in the pack. "Okay." She scooted off the picnic-table bench and started toward the Ford Taurus Riley had borrowed from the used-car lot.

He caught her halfway there, his hand encircling her elbow. "You should drive from here on. I'll get you to the starting point, then you can take it from there."

She took the keys he held out and unlocked the Taurus's driver door. She adjusted the seat and buckled herself in while he climbed in the passenger side.

"Just head northeast on this road and you'll come to Highway 287."

Hannah pulled the Taurus out of the rest area and back onto the main road, stealing a glance at Riley. He'd donned a pair of sunglasses and was gazing forward at the road, although he wore a slight smile that made her own lips curve in response.

A moment later, he cleared his throat. "I think Emily would have liked you."

Her smile faded. Forcing herself not to analyze that statement, she headed for Highway 287.

HE HAD TO STOP LETTING the mention of Emily's name paralyze him, he thought as he watched Hannah drive west on Highway 287. If not for himself, then for Emily. She'd be horrified to know he was trapped in her memory like a bug in amber. He'd never known a woman more alive, who'd found more joy in just living, than Emily, and she would hate what he'd become, almost as much as she'd loved him in life.

It was just—Hannah. Hannah made him feel things. Not just physical attraction. That was biological. He hadn't stopped being a man when Emily died. But those kinds of urges were no different than his stomach growling when he was hungry or yawning when he was sleepy.

Hannah made him laugh. She made him want to know more about her. She had the same sort of vibrancy, the same curiosity, the same enjoyment of the simple pleasures of life that had drawn him to Emily.

She was dangerous to him in the way that a simple biological response to a beautiful woman could never be.

She's leaving in less than a week, he reminded himself. There wasn't much point in trying to learn more about her or let himself worry about where their relationship was going to go.

Maybe that was as good an excuse as any to stop worrying and just enjoy what she was making him feel. Like a limb coming back to life after being asleep for a while, the worst of the painful tingles had begun to pass, and he was starting to feel a hum of energy that reminded him he wasn't dead after all.

He was thirty-four years old, in excellent health, with years of life ahead of him. It was time to start living again, wasn't it?

He knew what Emily would tell him.

"I got gas at that station," Hannah said, pointing to a Lassiter Oil station coming up on her left. Behind the station, a small herd of Appaloosas grazed on a dwindling patch of pastureland. "I'd forgotten about that. I filled up about fifteen minutes before I was pulled over."

"Are you sure this is the station?"

She nodded. "I remember the Appaloosas."

"Then we should stop here, too."

Hannah slowed and turned into the gas station, parking near the front. She shut off the engine. "I know I didn't go in. I paid at the pump. I think I got a couple of bottles of water out of one of those vending machines." She pointed to a pair of machines standing against the wall of the station's food mart.

Riley glanced at his watch. It was after three. According to the case report, she'd wrecked her car at Big Mike's Truck Stop, which was about ten miles down the highway.

"It takes about three or four minutes to fill up a tank. Did you talk to anyone?"

Her brow wrinkled as she considered the question. "I'm not sure—I don't really remember much about stopping here, except the horses. If there was someone else here filling up, I might have made small talk, but—"

He sighed. Her memory was still spotty from the concussion. Her doctor had admitted that she might never remember some of what happened that day.

"Let's get back on the road," he said after three minutes had passed.

She started the car, but paused a moment before putting it

into drive. "I think there was someone at the pumps. I kind of remember asking about the roads to Yellowstone—whether there'd been any closings yet. I don't remember the answer."

"It's okay," he assured her. "It probably doesn't have anything to do with what happened to you."

Still, he made a note to mention it to Joe. They could check the station's receipts from that day, maybe find out who else bought gas around the time she had.

They drove a little farther west. Riley tried to pay particular attention to the surroundings, as they should be coming up on wherever the attack had taken place any time now.

"Hmm," she murmured.

He looked up to find her brow furrowed. "What is it?"

"That road we just passed on the right. I think that may be where he was waiting."

Riley looked back toward the small dirt road they'd just passed. "You think he was waiting?"

"I check my mirrors regularly. Old habit my father drummed into me when he was teaching me to drive." She glanced at the mirror just then. "I think it was right about here when I looked into the rearview mirror and saw the blue lights."

He looked around them. There was no shoulder on the right to speak of; where the road top ended, the ground rose steeply up a craggy hillside.

"I couldn't pull over here," she said softly, her eyes narrowed as she followed the curve of the road. He noticed her breath was coming in short, fast little clips, even though her chin was up, her jaw squared with determination.

It was getting to her, being here.

"I was looking for—there." She pointed toward a turn-off ahead, where the shoulder widened enough to accommodate a vehicle. "That's where I pulled over. It happened there."

She slowed suddenly, whipping the Ford off the highway on to the side road. Braking at the road's edge, she jammed the Ford into Park and bent her head forward, her breath coming in short, shallow gasps.

He reached across and unbelted her. "Just breathe," he coaxed, rubbing her back. "Take a big breath and hold it for a count of ten."

She squeezed the steering wheel hard, breathing in and holding it while she counted to ten under her breath. She exhaled, then repeated the deep breath. Twice. Three times. One more deep breath and she looked at him, her eyes dark with humiliation. "Sorry about that."

"Don't be." He slid his hand up to her neck, gently kneading the tight muscles bunched beneath his fingers. He kept his voice calm and comforting. "Just take a minute to breathe."

After another minute, she was visibly calmer. But she couldn't quite bring herself to look him in the eye when she next spoke. "Any chance we could find tire tracks on the shoulder where he pulled me over?"

"I'll take a quick look, but we should probably call the Teton County Sheriff's Department. It's their case, officially. They'll want to call in the crime-scene investigators." He pulled his cell phone from the pocket of his jacket as he got out of the Ford and crossed to the highway to take a closer look at the shoulder.

What he found there made his heart sink.

There weren't any tire tracks at all. In fact, the sandy shoulder looked as if it had been raked clean of any marks either car might have made upon pulling over.

Son of a bitch was always a step ahead.

HANNAH RESTED HER HEAD against the back of the seat and watched the crime-scene investigators at work in her rearview mirror. They seemed to be taking soil samples, despite Riley's grim pronouncement earlier that someone had already tampered with the scene to remove any sort of tread marks that the police might have been able to preserve from the scene.

He'd sat with her awhile as they waited for the Teton County deputies to arrive but jumped from the car as soon as they drove up, no doubt as horrified by her humiliating bout of hysterics as she'd been.

She saw Riley moving away from the detectives overseeing the evidence collection. He opened the driver's door and held out his hand. "I'll drive home."

She took his hand and let him help her out of the car, her skin burning with embarrassment. He probably wasn't holding her weakness against her, she knew, but that didn't ease her own sense of shame. She was a Cooper, for God's sake. Coopers were made of tough stuff, and just because she was the only girl didn't mean it was okay to go all weak-kneed and neurotic.

"I'm not a wuss," she muttered aloud as she buckled herself into the passenger seat.

Riley turned to look at her. "I know that."

She slanted a look at him. He seemed to be sincere. "We don't have to leave now if you don't want to. I know you'd probably rather be back there with the other detectives."

"They're not going to find anything," Riley said with a brisk shake of his head. "They haven't found anything at the turn off down the road where you thought he might have lain in waiting, either. I think he covered his tracks." He gave a nod toward the western sky, where gunmetal rain clouds had started to gather. "Rain's coming. Let's not get stuck driving home in it." He took off his jacket, tossed it in the backseat of the borrowed car, and slid behind the wheel.

She settled back against the seat, willing herself to relax. Now that her brief panic attack had passed fully, the ebb of adrenaline had begun draining her body of energy. All she wanted to do at the moment was close her eyes and let the last of the tension melt away.

Riley fiddled with the radio dial until he found something soft and slow playing on a country station out of Jackson. The quiet music blended with the hum of the Ford's motor until the vibrations seemed to take over her weary body. Her limbs felt heavy and numb. The rain clouds blotted the afternoon sun from the sky, casting gloom across the Ford's dark interior, drawing her deeper into her own mind.

He was nearby. She felt him, like a chill in the air around her. She struggled to open her eyes, certain that if she looked in the side mirror, she'd see him lurking behind them, waiting to make his move.

She tried to warn Riley, but her voice came out in a soft, voiceless cry. Her arms and legs felt paralyzed, and a growing hum filled her ears.

He was closer. She could smell him, the fetid stench of hate and malice, stronger than the sting of pepper spray that still seemed to linger in her nose. Was he right outside her window? If she opened her eyes, would she find him staring back at her, from a face she had struggled for two days to picture? Or would she see nothing but those hard, cruel hands, reaching for her, determined to finish what he'd started two days ago?

Hard hands grabbed her from behind and squeezed her throat, trapping her breath in her chest. Her head started pounding, and the world around her swirled into a spiral of darkness.

Oh, my God he's here, he's in the car, I'm going to die—

"Hannah!"

The fingers lost their grip. Air rushed into her lungs, and she lurched forward, her paralysis gone. Her surroundings swam into focus. The dashboard in front of her. Fast breathing beside her.

She had to get out.

Fumbling with the seat-belt buckle, she managed to free herself just as someone grabbed her arm. She jerked away, plucking at the door handle, a soft keening sob escaping her lungs as she missed on the first try. On the second attempt, the door opened and she flung herself out of the car into the driving rain, scrambling over the rocky shoulder.

"Hannah!"

She kept moving, though her sluggish brain tried to process how the killer knew her name. And what was he doing in the car?

She heard swift footsteps on the ground behind her, and her heart rate soared. Hands caught at her, missing at first but finally trapping her in their hard grip. She struggled to get away, but strong arms wrapped around her, pulling her tight against a warm, solid body.

"Hannah, it's Riley. Stop fighting me."

She fought a few seconds longer until his words seeped into her sleep-addled brain. She twisted around to look at him, needing to see his face, to be sure.

Rain dripped off the brim of his hat, falling against her cheek. Beneath the brim, his anxious blue eyes bored into hers. "Are you okay?" His voice shook.

Relief flooded her body, knocking her off balance. She grasped his arms, her fingers digging in just to keep herself from sliding to the ground.

He caught her up against him. "You were trying to scream in the car," he said, his voice rough.

"I thought he was here." Her voice came out in a croak. "I thought he was trying to kill me."

Riley's eyes closed as he took a couple of quick, deep breaths. "I didn't know if you were having some sort of seizure or something. I pulled over and then you just went wild."

He had parked the Ford off the side of the road, she saw, on a narrow shoulder not far from the exit to the rest area where they'd eaten lunch and played that silly game of popsmack. She must have slept longer than she realized; they'd been back on the road for almost an hour and a half.

"It felt real," she said, tears stinging her eyes. She'd felt the man's anger. His hate.

"Nobody's out there," he assured her, pushing her wet hair out of her face. His hand lingered against her cheek, his touch warm and firm, full of strength tempered by gentle concern. Her breath hitched, catching somewhere in the middle of her chest. She gazed up into his shadowed eyes, where something glittered, fierce and white hot, stealing the air from her lungs. His fingers tangled in the hair at her temples, trapping her.

He was going to kiss her. And she was going to let him.

As she rose to meet him, his mouth descended, hard and hungry against hers.

Chapter Nine

Though a cold wind whipped around them, and the rain drenched them to the skin, all Hannah could feel was Riley's mouth over hers, hard and relentless, drawing out of her a feverish passion she thought she'd buried somewhere so deep inside it could never be found again. She dug her fingers into the muscles of his arms, holding on tightly as he dragged her closer to him, until her breasts pressed flat against the hard wall of his chest, until she could feel his heartbeat galloping wildly alongside her own.

Slowly, he ran his hand over her jaw, down the curve of her neck, his thumb settling on the hollow of her throat. His mouth softened, coaxing her to relax against him. His tongue slid lightly over her bottom lip, seducing her until she opened up to him, letting him deepen the kiss.

Their tongues met briefly, a gentle thrust and parry, and a low moan escaped her throat.

The sound seemed to catch him off guard. He went still, his mouth resting briefly against hers, then letting go. His hand dropped from her neck and away from her body altogether.

Released from his hold, she had to struggle to keep her feet, her breath coming in short, raspy pants.

"I'm sorry," he said, his voice tight.

She didn't know what to say. Was he sorry for kissing her in the first place? Sorry for pulling away and leaving her breathless and stunned?

"You scared me," he added, immediately wincing as if he knew it was the wrong thing to say.

The sudden tension between them was almost painful. She pressed the heel of her hand against her suddenly aching forehead. "Let's get back in the car, okay? We're soaked."

He gave a brisk nod and guided her back to the car. He opened the door for her, letting her settle in before he shut it and went around to the driver's side. He cranked the engine and turned up the heat, pulling back out on to the highway.

The next hour passed in near silence, the beat of the windshield wipers and the patter of rain taking up the slack.

They reached Canyon Creek near nightfall, stopping at the used-car lot to switch vehicles. On the short drive back to Riley's place, he broke the silence only to make a phone call to the office. "He's not in? Do you know where he went?"

After listening a moment longer, he rang off, gazing ahead at the road with his brow furrowed.

"What is it?" Hannah asked.

"Joe left the office about four hours ago, headed for the Grand Teton National Park. He didn't leave any message for me."

"Maybe it's not related to my case?"

He shook his head. "Grand Teton is way out of our jurisdiction. Why would he be going there?"

Hannah had a sinking feeling they'd find out sooner rather than later.

JACK'S TRUCK WAS NOWHERE in sight when Riley pulled the Silverado up the gravel-packed drive to his house. He frowned, wondering where his brother-in-law was off to in this storm.

As Hannah started to get out of the truck, he put his hand out to hold her in place. "Let me go get an umbrella for you."

She stared at him as if he'd lost his mind. "I'm already drenched to the bone. I'm not going to melt." She slid out of the car into the rain.

He hurried to catch up with her, unlocking the door and guiding her to the narrow mudroom just off the kitchen. He took her jacket and shook off the water, hanging it to finish drying on a hook on the wall. He did the same with his own jacket, trying to ignore the tense silence that had fallen between them.

What the hell had gotten into him, grabbing her up like that, kissing her with all the finesse of a cowboy hitting town after weeks on the trail? Jack, for God's sake, would have handled her with a more gentleness, and he was a damned bull rider and an unrepentant player.

Hannah crossed the kitchen to stand near the wood stove. Inside the chamber, the embers were dying, but it still gave off a soft stream of heat. Riley joined her there, holding his hands out to warm them from the damp chill.

"Hannah, I wanted to say—"

"Do you think Joe might have left a message on your answering machine?" she interrupted, looking up at him with anxious eyes.

That should have been the first thing he thought about, he realized with some chagrin. He went down the hall to his bedroom to check, acutely aware of Hannah's soft footsteps moving down the hallway behind him.

There was nothing on his answering machine, and when he tried calling Joe's cell phone, he got no answer.

"Something's wrong, isn't it?" Hannah's voice was right behind him. He turned to find her standing quietly, her eyes dark with worry.

"I don't know," he admitted, touching her arm, needing that contact to ground him, somehow.

She laid her hand on his chest, right over his heart, her touch gentle and questioning. He put his own hand over hers, pulling her into a gentle, undemanding embrace.

They stood there a long time, wrapped in each other's arms, her head resting against his shoulder. Outside the house, darkness fell, painting the bedroom with shadows. The only light came from the glowing embers of the wood stove in the corner, yet Riley couldn't seem to rouse himself to release Hannah and go turn on the overhead light.

"I'm sure he's okay," she murmured against his shirt.

"It's unusual for him not to answer his phone."

"Maybe it's out of cell-tower range or something."

That was certainly possible. There were plenty of places in the Wyoming hills and valleys where cell-phone towers didn't reach. And had Joe left Riley a message, telling him he might be out of pocket for the afternoon, he probably wouldn't give it a second thought.

"Should I call Jane and see if she knows where he is?"

"No," Hannah said quickly, pulling her head back to look at him. "You'd just worry her without really knowing anything. Give Joe time to get home and try him again later." She let go of him, backing out of the embrace, though this time she didn't seem uncomfortable to be around him. "Let's get out of these wet clothes and then see what we can rustle up for dinner. I bet you'll hear from Joe by the time we're finished."

She was almost right. Riley had just walked into the kitchen, dressed in a dry pair of jeans and a warm sweatshirt when a knock sounded on the back door. A second later, Joe stuck his head through the door. "Riley?"

"Come on in," he answered, turning as Hannah came into the kitchen from the hallway. She'd dressed in a loose-fitting pair of yoga pants and an oversized T-shirt, and still he found himself wanting to pin her up against the kitchen wall and finish what he'd started out on that rain-washed highway.

He dragged his gaze away as Joe let himself into the kitchen, rain dripping from his Stetson to the floor of the entryway. He gave them both an odd look as he ducked into the mudroom briefly to hang up his wet coat, then returned to the kitchen where they waited.

"I heard you went to Grand Teton," Riley said, trying not to sound impatient.

Joe nodded. "I got a call from Jim Tanner. A hiker found a body up there."

Next to Riley, Hannah moved sideways, dropping into one of the nearby kitchen chairs. Riley slanted a look at her to make sure she was okay. She looked a little pale, but her gaze was steady as she waited for Joe to elaborate.

"They found pepper spray on her skin. She was wrapped in a plastic sheet and dumped in a creek just inside the park east of Moran. She's been dead less than a day. Maybe as little as a couple of hours. M.E. thinks the hikers found her within minutes of her being dumped."

Riley shook his head. "Our guy's not that sloppy."

"Who else could it be?" Hannah asked. "It can't be a copycat, since none of that stuff is common knowledge, right?"

Riley looked at her, then back at Joe, not yet sure what to think. Their guy wasn't the sloppy type, so if this was him, something in his MO had changed.

"He could be escalating, beyond his normal control," Joe sug-

The Reader Service — Here's how it works:

BUSINESS REPLY MAIL

FIRST-CLASS MAIL   PERMIT NO. 717   BUFFALO, NY

POSTAGE WILL BE PAID BY ADDRESSEE

THE READER SERVICE
PO BOX 1867
BUFFALO NY 14240-9952

NO POSTAGE
NECESSARY
IF MAILED
IN THE
UNITED STATES

gested. "Maybe he couldn't handle the failure of letting Hannah slip through his fingers not once but twice in the last two days."

It was possible, Riley supposed, but something about that theory just didn't feel right. The guy had been able not only to escape capture for the last three years but escape detection as well. Riley had been the first law-enforcement officer in Wyoming to connect the dots, and even he'd had doubts at first. Was a guy as wily as that really going to lose control and start getting sloppy because one of his targets got away?

"Maybe it's not escalation," Hannah said. Riley looked at her and found her gazing back at him, her green eyes dark with horror. "Maybe it was a message. To me. What he'd have done to me if I hadn't gotten away."

Riley pulled out the chair beside Hannah and sat down, reaching across to close his hand over hers where it lay on the table. "Don't you start blaming yourself for this."

Joe sat across from them. "Riley's right. Whatever this bastard does, it's his own doing. You haven't done a damned thing wrong."

Riley squeezed her hand. "What were you supposed to have done differently—let him kill you?"

"No, of course not," she said, releasing a deep sigh. "I just think he's trying to tell us we can't stop him. I mean—he killed her and dumped her in a national park where hikers found her probably within minutes. That's bold."

"And risky, too," Joe pointed out. "If he starts thinking he's invincible, that's good for us. He'll start making mistakes, and we'll have him."

"Are we going to be in the loop on this investigation?" Riley asked Joe. "I need to see the reports."

"They're faxing everything they get. As soon as they know something, we'll know something. I'll bring by copies when they're ready." Joe shot a comforting smile at Hannah. "Don't let this get to you, Hannah. You just stay safe here with Riley and do what you can to remember more about the attack. That's all you can do."

Riley walked him to the door when he rose to leave. "Do you think she's right? Is it a message?"

"I think you and Hannah need to keep working on her memory lapses," Joe responded. "If she knows anything at all about the attack she hasn't yet remembered, it could be the break we need. If this guy is willing to kill someone just to let us know he can, nobody's safe."

Riley closed the door behind Joe and looked back at Hannah, who still sat at the table, gazing at him with wide, worried eyes. "Why don't we rustle up some dinner?" he suggested.

"I'm not hungry."

He sighed. He wasn't, either, even though lunch had been a long time ago. He wished he knew where Jack was. It had been a real help to have him around for the past day, especially since the horses didn't just feed themselves every day. He should have asked Joe to take over stable duties that night, but Joe had a very pregnant wife at home, and with a murderous bastard out there killing women—

"I should call Jack," he said aloud, reaching into his pocket for his phone. "I'm not sure whether he fed the horses or not."

"We could do that, couldn't we?" Hannah stood, flexing her arms over her head. "I wouldn't mind the exercise."

Or the distraction, he suspected. "You sure? It's cold and wet out there."

"I go fishing in December in the rain all the time," she said firmly, her square little chin lifting. "I'm not fragile."

He didn't remind her of how she'd damned near fallen apart earlier that afternoon. Post-traumatic stress could fell big, tough, well-trained men. Then again, considering what she'd been through, she was holding up pretty well.

"Okay," he agreed. He grabbed their coats from the mud-room and led her out to the truck.

THE HARD RAIN HADN'T SEEMED to affect the hard-pressed dirt track to the stable, Hannah noticed. Perhaps the ground had been too dry for the rain to have made much impact, or maybe it was mostly rocky soil to begin with. There was a lot about Wyoming that seemed almost as alien to her as a foreign country, from the craggy mountains to the thin, dry air.

Amazing, then, how familiar Riley seemed to her after such a short time. Though she knew so little about him, beyond the handful of facts she'd gleaned over the past two days, she was more convinced than ever that she'd made the right choice that night in the hospital when she'd made the leap of faith and put herself under his protection.

He put her to work, showing no signs of trying to coddle her. She was grateful for the show of confidence. After the way she'd acted during their trip west that day, he'd have been justified in thinking she was weak and unreliable.

She brushed the mud off the chestnut mare's coat and held her bridle while Riley picked the dirt out of her hooves. "What's her name?" she asked.

"This is Bella. She was Emily's." Riley stood up and patted the mare's flank. "The black gelding is Jazz. And those two—" he pointed to the paint gelding and the buckskin mare they'd already settled for the night "—are Lucky and Lady. Joe bought them last year after he and Jane married. He doesn't have a stable on his land, so we share feed costs and vet bills, and he pays me for boarding them. He and Jane used to come daily to ride, too, before Jane got pregnant."

"I mentioned we've been thinking about building a stable on our land back home, to offer trail riding up the mountain as part of our services, didn't I?" Hannah put the brush back on the tack table and turned to look at Riley. "We all know how to ride well, and I think my brother Luke might consider coming back home to run the stable if we ever got around to doing it. He's the best horseman among us."

"I thought all your family was together back home in Alabama." Riley put Bella in her stall and added food to her feed bowl.

"We mostly are. Sam and his little girl Maddy live in the Washington, D.C. area—he's a prosecutor—but he's been talking about moving back to Alabama so Maddy can grow up around her grandparents and her cousins. If he comes back, the only one missing will be Luke. He retired from the Marines last year, but so far, he's still hanging around San Diego." She couldn't hide a little frown.

Riley picked up on it immediately. "That worries you?"

"A little," she admitted. She turned to look at Bella over the stall door. The mare was crunching her feed contentedly, her dark eyes soft and calm. "Luke has always been a bit of a loner, which is hard to do in a family as big as ours, but after his last tour of duty, it's—worse, somehow. He hardly ever calls, and when we call, he keeps it short."

"Is he married? Or maybe has a girlfriend keeping him busy?"

She smiled. "I wish. I think I'd relax more if that's what I thought it was. There's just—I don't know. It almost feels like he's brooding about something."

"Do you think something happened to him that he's not telling you?"

She wasn't sure. She knew he'd done a tour of duty in Kaziristan right before he returned stateside, but that had been nothing but peacekeeping. Kaziristan's civil war had been over for a couple of years now, and the small Central Asian republic was mostly stable. Compared to some of his previous tours of duty, the one in Kaziristan should have been a cakewalk.

"I just want him back home where I can keep an eye on him," she answered finally.

Riley smiled. "All your ducks in a row."

"Exactly." She laughed self-consciously. "I can't believe I just told you all that about Luke. I haven't even talked to my parents about it."

"Maybe it's easier to tell things like that to a stranger."

Except he didn't feel like a stranger, she thought. She looked up at him, realizing just how much she was going to miss him when she had to go home.

And every day took her closer to that moment.

"What if I don't remember more about who attacked me?" she asked aloud.

The sound of boots on the hard-packed barn floor made them both turn in surprise. Jack Drummond stood in the doorway, his hat and jacket glistening with rain. He looked from Hannah to Riley, his expression dark and suspicious.

"Someone attacked you?" he asked.

Hannah and Riley exchanged looks. He gave a little shake of his head, clearly not ready to let Jack in on their secret.

"We were wondering where you'd gotten off to," Hannah said quickly, ignoring Jack's question. "Did you have fun in town?"

Riley stepped up behind her and slipped his arms around her, clasping his hands in front of her stomach and resting his cheek against her head. "*You* were wondering, baby," he said in a low growl that seemed to make her bones liquefy.

"Don't try to distract me." Jack strode into the stable, his eyes darkening. "You said something about an attack,

Hannah." He reached inside his jacket and pulled out a folded section of newspaper. "Funny—I read something about an attack in the newspaper just this afternoon."

Riley's arms tightened around Hannah's waist. His tension radiated through her where their bodies touched, making her stomach clench painfully.

"Seems a woman was attacked on the road to Moran the other day. No identity given, but police sources say the assailant got away, and other sources mentioned a possible second attack in a Jackson hospital." Jack handed the paper to Hannah. "Page three."

She opened the paper to the page he mentioned. There it was: *Tourist attacked on highway; hospital security breach?*

"What makes you think that's me?"

"The timing. Your injuries. The complete impossibility of Riley meeting someone online, much less someone he'd invite to stay with him after just one meeting."

Riley dropped his hands away from Hannah, backing away. Cool air replaced the heat of his body, and she shivered.

"Nobody can know Hannah's connected to that story. Nobody, Jack. Understand?"

Jack's lips tightened to a thin, angry line. "You lied to me. *Me,* Riley. I didn't deserve that."

"You drink too much, Jack. You party too much. You don't keep your tongue when you're drinking."

Real pain etched lines in Jack's face. "That's what you think of me?"

"Tell me it's not true."

"It's not true," Jack said angrily. Then he lowered his voice. "Not anymore."

Riley's expression grew thoughtful. "When did that happen?"

"Last year. I got drunk in Amarillo and lost the best thing

that ever happened to me." Jack removed his hat and ran his fingers briskly through his thick black hair. "I guess you wouldn't have known about that."

"And why's that, Jack? Because you haven't been back here since Emily died?"

"I couldn't."

Hannah felt like a voyeur, watching the two men deal with their private pain. She eased away from them, retreating to the horse box near the back, where Lucky quietly chewed what was left of the night's feed. She ran her hand down his brown spotted neck. He rewarded her with a soft nicker of pleasure.

"Why did you bring her here to stay with you?" Jack asked, apparently not caring that she was right there in the stable with them. "She could have stayed with Joe and his wife, or, hell, the Teton County Sheriff's Department could've found her a safe place to stay. Why was the first lie you came up with about sleeping with her? Have you given that any thought?"

"Stop it, Jack! This is all about Emily," Riley said, his voice rising with emotion. "Everything I've done since the day she died is about making sure the son of a bitch who murdered her gets what's coming to him. Don't you dare question that."

Hannah felt a sick, hot pain in the center of her chest. She turned her back to them, pressing her face against the gelding's warm, silky neck.

What's the matter, Hannah? You knew what was what. You knew it all along.

"Okay, so nobody can know why she's here," Jack said. "What's next?"

Hannah looked over her shoulder at Riley, wondering what he'd answer. He paused, as if at a loss for an answer, and slowly turned to look at her, his expression impossible to read.

"A lot of people have already seen us together," he said,

his gaze remaining locked with hers. "The few who've asked, I told the same story I told you, Jack. It's probably all over town by now. We can't shift gears now."

"I can move back to the guest room," she suggested, pleased that her voice came out calm and pragmatic, considering how much she wanted to go find a quiet corner and cry.

"Then I guess I should go," Jack said.

"No," Hannah said quickly, moving toward him. The last thing she could bear was driving Jack away from what was apparently the only home—and family—he had.

And the last thing she needed was to spend the next few nights alone in the house with Riley.

Chapter Ten

Quiet tension settled over the scene, punctuated by the drumming of rain on the stable's metal roof. Hannah's pulse drummed in her ears as she waited for Jack's answer.

Jack looked at Riley, a question in his eyes. Hannah looked at Riley, too, wondering what he'd say.

"It's your home," Riley said. "You're Emily's brother."

She released a soft breath and laid her hand on Jack's arm. "You keep the guest room. I'll bunk on the sofa."

"I'll take the couch. You're still recuperating." Jack patted her hand, the tension in his muscles easing. "Dinner's on the table. I grabbed takeout from Haley's Barbecue—best beef ribs west of the Mississippi."

The thought of food made her feel ill, but she managed a smile. "Why don't you drive me back to the house and I'll brew up some old-fashioned Southern sweet tea to go with it? Riley can finish up here."

"Wait and let me drive you back," Riley countered.

"Don't you trust me?" Jack shot him a pointed look.

Riley frowned. "Fine. But don't mess around. Go straight home and lock up when you get there."

Jack laid his hand on Hannah's back, gentle pressure guiding her out with him. They dashed through the rain to his battered Ford F-10 and hurried into the cab.

Jack paused with his hand on the starter. "I know I'm being a big baby about all this. It's just—Riley was the best thing that ever happened to Emily. It's hard even imagining him caring about anyone else the way he loved her, you know?"

Hannah smiled, genuinely this time. "I do understand. And for the record—I think Emily was the best thing that ever happened to him, too. I know he thinks so."

The gratitude in Jack's eyes made her want to cry. "I wish you could have known her."

"I do, too," she admitted.

Emily Patterson must have been one hell of a woman, to have left such a big hole in the lives of men like Jack Drummond and Riley Patterson.

HANNAH HAD THOUGHT SHE'D be relieved by having a room to herself after so much togetherness with Riley over the past couple of days, but she'd found it hard to fall asleep. Every bump, rattle or moan of the wind kept her on edge for most of the night. She fell into a restless sleep around 3:00 a.m., waking around seven thanks to the sound of bootfalls outside her door. Her headache was back, though she suspected the culprit was her sleepless night rather than her concussion, and sometime in the night the fire in her wood stove had died away, leaving the room icy cold.

She dressed in jeans and a dark green sweater, thankful she'd done her homework and packed for the cooler mountain climate. Back home in Alabama, early October was still warm enough to walk around in short sleeves and sandals most days.

She followed the smell of bacon and coffee to the kitchen

and found Jack alone at the stove, cobbling together an omelet. "Good morning," he said over his shoulder.

She mumbled a response and poured a cup of coffee, stirring in a teaspoon of sugar from a canister by the coffeemaker. The brew was hot and strong, just like she liked it. She took her cup back to the table and let it warm her up.

"Want an omelet?"

Now that the coffee was doing the trick, her appetite was kicking in. "Yes, please. Where's Riley?"

"Joe came by early this morning. I think they're out with the horses." Jack flipped an omelet onto a plate and placed it in front of her. "Dig in."

The omelet was excellent, and she told him so.

"Don't sound so surprised," he said mildly.

"I just figured a rodeo cowboy wouldn't have much time to hone his culinary skills."

"Oh, there's plenty of downtime. And rodeo pay is pretty unpredictable, so you learn to get by without a lot of the perks." He finished off his double omelet quickly, downing it with two cups of coffee. "I'm getting too old for it."

"Thinking about settling down?" she teased, expecting him to quickly deny it.

But he didn't. "I've lost too much time with people I love while I was chasing rodeos around the country. Maybe if I'd been here—"

She reached across the table and covered his hand with hers. "From what I understand, there's not much anyone could have done, except stop the killer first."

He turned his palm up, squeezing her hand with a grateful half smile. "You're right. I know you are. I just—"

He fell quiet when the kitchen door opened and Riley entered, Joe Garrison bringing up the rear.

Riley's eyes narrowed slightly as he saw Hannah's hand in Jack's. Hannah ignored the urge to jerk her hand away, letting Jack remove his hand first.

"Anything new?" she asked, directing the question to Joe. Riley crossed silently to the coffeemaker and poured a cup.

Joe sat next to her, laying a thick folder on the table. "Maybe. We're not sure." He opened the folder and handed her a photocopy of a driver's license. "Does this man look familiar?"

The man in question was Dale Morton, age 44, with a home address in Moran, Wyoming. He had sandy-brown hair and, according to the information on the license, brown eyes, though it was hard to tell that from the photo. He was average-looking, maybe a little on the beefy side.

She shook her head. "But I didn't see his face."

"As far as you remember." Riley had remained standing to drink his coffee, leaning against the counter. He continued to watch her through narrowed eyes.

It was starting to annoy her.

"Who is this guy?"

"He's a security guard at the hospital. He was on duty the night you were admitted, but he was off duty earlier in the day. He also worked at the hospital in Casper where Emily was working when she was murdered," Riley answered.

Jack reached across the table to take the photo from Hannah's hands. "You think this is the guy who killed Em?"

"We don't know," Joe warned quickly. "We were looking for links, and that one turned up."

"It's the only link between the two hospitals among the Jackson Memorial security staff," Riley added.

"What if it wasn't someone in security?" Hannah asked. "I mean, we don't know that it wasn't someone on the medical staff. Whoever it was sure seemed to know his way around an IV tube."

"We started with security because of the tampered surveillance recording," Joe said. "We're looking at the medical staff, too."

"Joe just wanted to pass this one by you, see if he jogged your memory at all."

She looked up at Jack. He handed her the photo again, and she gave it another look. "I think the build could probably fit." Though she'd seen little more than the man's midsection, he'd been on the bigger side. Not overweight, exactly, but thick waisted and on the burly side.

"I'll tell Sheriff Tanner. Maybe we can connect him to some of the other crime scenes." Joe took the photo from her and put it back in the file.

"Nothing yet on the belt buckle?" she asked.

"No, but we've got people from three different agencies out there looking," Joe assured her. He picked up the file and stood. "I've got to get to the office. I'll call later if anything new comes up." He let himself out.

"There's an omelet for you in the pan on the stove," Jack told Riley.

Riley made a grunting sound in response and grabbed a clean plate from the drying rack by the sink. He transferred the omelet to the plate, took the seat Joe had vacated and started eating without a word.

Jack caught Hannah's eye, lifting one eyebrow.

She shrugged.

"If you're going to talk about me, do it aloud," Riley said, setting his fork down by his plate.

"Bad morning out at the stable?" Jack asked innocently.

"No, everything's fine. I just didn't sleep well."

"I didn't, either," Hannah admitted. "The coffee helped."

Riley looked at her, his expression softening. "You didn't have to get up so early."

"I don't want to sleep away what time I have left here in Wyoming. I feel like I haven't accomplished anything."

"You have," he assured her. "We may not find the guy before you leave, but you've already given us leads we didn't have before."

"I wish I could remember more details. Maybe something about the car, or his voice or—something."

Riley finished his omelet and washed it down with the rest of his coffee. "Actually, I thought about that while I was trying to go to sleep. I think we may have been doing the wrong things to try to jog your memory."

"What do you mean?"

"The only thing you've really remembered was the belt buckle. And that happened when you weren't actually trying to remember, right?"

She nodded, her cheeks growing warm as she remembered the intimacy of that moment, alone in Riley's bedroom. He'd been sitting there watching her, close enough to touch.

"It gave me an idea." Riley's voice took on a dark, warm color that left her with no doubt that he also remembered that moment between them. He held out his hand, his gaze challenging her to take it.

She put her hand in his and rose from the table.

"Jack, you don't mind cleaning up, do you?" Riley didn't wait for an answer, closing his fingers around Hannah's and leading her to the back door. He reached into the mudroom and grabbed their jackets off the hooks, letting go of her hand just long enough to help her into her coat.

Taking her hand again, he led her outside.

"Feel like a little exercise?" he asked, waving toward a wooden post to the right of the door, where Jazz and Bella stood, saddled and a little restless, breath rising from their nostrils in wispy curls of white.

She grinned, her mood immediately lightening. "We're going riding?"

"You bet." He handed her Bella's reins, and she pulled herself up in the saddle. The chestnut mare nickered softly, her muscles twitching as if eager for a good run.

Riley mounted Jazz and took the lead, guiding the horses through an open gate toward the pasture beyond the stables. Once they were out in the pasture, he gave Jazz a swift nudge in the side and the shiny black gelding sprinted ahead, hitting a full, joyous gallop in a matter of seconds.

Excitement flowing like blood in her veins, Hannah urged Bella into a run and flew across the pasture in pursuit.

"THAT DOES IT," SHE SAID LATER, watching the horses grazing a short distance away, their coats glistening with a light sweat after the morning run. "We're definitely adding trail rides to the Cooper Cove Outdoor Experience."

Riley had led them to the upper reaches of the pasture, where the grassland met the foot of Sawyer's Rise. Flat, wide boulders dotted the area, providing a dry place to sit after the exhilarating ride.

"You're a good rider." Riley settled next to her on the boulder rather than finding his own seat on one of the nearby rocks, though her choice of seats was barely big enough for two. She didn't know whether to be glad for his warmth or worried by the sudden acceleration of her pulse.

"I'm no cowgirl." She smiled to cover her sudden nerves. "Bella's a great horse."

"She likes you." He reached up and combed his fingers through her tousled hair. "We need to find you a hat."

She closed her eyes, trying hard not to lean into his light touch. She might as well stop kidding herself—she was halfway over the moon about this guy, and all the self-lectures in the world wouldn't do a damned bit of good.

So what if they'd be parting ways forever in just a few days? People had vacation flings all the time. Would it really be so wrong to enjoy whatever there was between them, even if she knew it could never last? Once she got home, she could file it away as a nice memory, to take out now and then and remember with fondness.

Couldn't she?

Riley's fingers crept lower, moving gently against the muscles of her neck. "How's your head? Any more pain or dizziness?"

"No," she answered. The headache she'd awakened with was long gone, banished by the invigorating ride. She felt better than she had since the attack. "You don't have to treat me like an invalid anymore. I really feel fine now."

He shifted until his legs were on either side of her and added his other hand to the neck massage. "I wouldn't have brought you riding with me if I didn't know that."

Giving up her resistance, she relaxed back against his chest and gave herself permission to enjoy being close to him.

"Too bad we don't have a deck of cards with us," he murmured in her ear. "We could play another game of smackpop."

"Popsmack," she corrected with a chuckle. "We don't need cards—we could just take turns. You can start. Ask me anything."

"Anything?"

She nodded. "Except how much I weigh."

"I already know. I peeked at your hospital chart."

She groaned. "Completely unfair."

He tugged at her hair. "Can I ask a question or not?"

She sighed and settled back against him. "Shoot."

"Does the Crappie Queen have to wear a crown?"

She nudged him with her elbow. "Smart aleck."

"And maybe one of those—what do you call it—sashes?"

"It wasn't like I was in a pageant or anything," she protested. "I'm just the best crappie fisherman on Gossamer Lake. I know where all the little suckers are hiding, no matter what time of year."

She felt his lips nuzzle her earlobe. "Do you wear little shorts when you fish?"

"Only in the summer," she murmured, moving her head to make it easier for him to keep doing whatever amazing thing it was he was doing to the side of her neck. "And that's two questions."

"Sorry. Your turn."

She pondered what to ask, not wanting anything to shatter this perfect moment of contentment. She could keep it light, she supposed, like he had. Something he could answer yes or no, so he wouldn't have to remove his lips from the side of her neck for long.

Before she had a chance to speak, however, Riley's cell phone rang. Relaxation was over; Riley stood, stepping around the boulder as he answered. "Hey, Joe, what's up?"

As he listened to Joe's response, his expression darkened. He shot a quick look at Hannah. "We'll be right there."

"What's happened?" she asked when he rang off.

His expression went grim. "Someone's leaked your name to the press."

THE FIRST FLUSH OF ALARM had passed quickly on the ride back to the house, settling into a low-level sense of tension by the time she and Riley found Joe waiting in the den.

Joe didn't waste time on the niceties. "A reporter from a Casper TV station who works out of Jackson Hole broke the story. They have your name and some of the details of the attack."

"How?" Riley asked tersely.

"He says an anonymous source, but it almost has to be someone from the hospital. I think Jim Tanner runs too tight a ship for it to be anyone from his department."

"Could have been an EMT," Riley suggested. "They were first on the scene, had access to her driver's license. Someone could have greased somebody's palm."

"Why is it even a story?" Hannah asked, torn between anxiety and confusion. "I'm nobody famous. I didn't even get hurt that much."

"You're a tourist," Joe answered. "If someone's out there attacking tourists, this close to two national parks—"

"It's news," Hannah finished for him.

"How much do they know about the attack?" Riley asked.

"Less than we do. No mention of the cop-car angle, and of course, nobody's connected it to any of the other murders, although I'm beginning to think it's only a matter of time before someone puts two and two together and realizes that the murder at Grand Teton is connected."

"That's odd, isn't it?" Something tugged at the back of her mind. "The anonymous source didn't think to add the part about the fake cop car. I mean, that would be a pretty sensational detail to omit."

"Maybe the leaker didn't know that detail," Joe said.

"Or he didn't want the press to know," Hannah replied.

Both men turned to look at her.

"What if the killer is the one who leaked the information?" she asked.

Riley's expression darkened. "To flush you out?"

"Using the press to do it," Joe added.

"Half the town knows Hannah's here by now," Riley said in alarm. "We need to move her somewhere else."

"No," Hannah said firmly. An idea was clicking into place in her brain, perfect and terrible.

"No?" Riley looked at her as if she'd lost her mind.

"He wants to flush me out, right?"

"Looks that way," Riley agreed warily.

She lifted her chin. "Then let him."

Chapter Eleven

Riley turned abruptly toward Hannah, ceasing his rapid pacing. The stubborn set of her jaw, which he generally found appealing, had started to get on his nerves over the last half hour, as he and Joe had tried in vain to talk her out of her dangerous, hare-brained idea. "That's it. You're not doing it. Discussion over."

Next to him, Joe took a deep, swift breath. He gave Riley a warning look that Riley ignored.

"You're not my keeper," Hannah retorted, crossing closer and coming to a stop in front of him. Her eyes blazed with green fire. "You don't order me around."

Riley looked over at Joe, completely at a loss. "Tell her it's a bad idea."

"I've spent the last thirty minutes doing just that," Joe reminded him. "But she's right. It's her choice. Even if it's wrong," he added sternly, giving Hannah a look of pure frustration.

"I don't have a lot of time left to help you catch this guy, and I don't know how I'm supposed to go back to my nice, safe life in Alabama if I don't do everything I can to stop that monster from killing another woman." Her expression softened, her green eyes pleading with Riley to understand. "Emily would do the same thing, wouldn't she?"

He pressed his lips together, biting back a harsher retort. "That's below the belt, Hannah." He slanted a look at Joe, who got the message and headed out of the den to give them some privacy.

Her expression softened more. "I'm sorry. I just need you to understand."

He closed his hands around her arms, desperate to make her see what she was asking of him. "I understand. But I don't think you do."

"I lost Emily three years ago this week," he said, trying not to let too much of his emotion spill over into his words. He wasn't looking for her pity. He wanted her to understand the stakes. "She wasn't doing anything crazy, just driving home from work, and suddenly she just wasn't there anymore. Everything we'd built together was gone, in a heartbeat."

She lifted her hand to his face, her palm warm and soft against his jaw. "I'm sorry."

"I don't want you to be sorry. I want you to see that I don't need this bastard to kill someone else I care about."

Moisture pooled in her eyes. "I don't think it has to be that risky," she answered. "Listen—we already know he's taking more risks than he usually does, or he wouldn't have killed the woman near Moran. I'm the one who got away, and it's driving him crazy."

She took his hand in hers, drawing him with her to the sofa. They sat together, silent for a minute, as if they'd mutually agreed to let their passions cool so they could talk more reasonably.

She folded his hand between hers, her grip gentle but firm.

"He's the one who's out of control. If he really did tip off the press, he's the one taking a risk. The reporter he talked to knows who he is."

"He's not going to burn his source."

"It doesn't matter. It was still a risk, and the killer took it because he can't stand that I'm the one who got away. I'm the one who was smarter than he was. That's how he sees it. He can't let that stand."

"What makes you think we can do this thing safely?"

"We hold all the cards. We know he's after me. We're on alert. He's the one taking stupid chances."

Riley pulled his hand away from hers and stood. "No. It's not worth the risk." He paced away from her, a bleak resolve stiffening his back. No way in hell would he let her put herself in the kind of danger she was talking about. There was only one choice left. One he hated more than he ever imagined he would. But it was the best way to keep her safe.

He turned and took in the sight of her slowly, thoroughly. Committing her to memory. When he spoke, his voice was tinged with regret but full of calm resolve.

"It's time for you to go home, Hannah."

"YOU'RE GOING TO LEAVE A MARK." Jack took the grooming brush from Hannah's hand and patted Bella's side. They were alone in the stable; Joe and Riley were back at the house, talking about new strategies for going after the killer without Hannah's involvement.

She'd made her escape to the stable soon after Riley's calm announcement that her time in Wyoming was over, using the horses as an excuse to get away from him before she said something she'd regret.

"He's not trying to get rid of you, you know."

She knew. She'd seen the regret in Riley's eyes. Somehow that only made things worse.

"And for what it's worth, I think you're right about talking to the press." Jack handed the brush back to her. "If we have a chance to catch that monster—"

Hannah touched his arm, knowing that his need to catch the killer was even greater than her own.

"What are you going to do now?" A thoughtful look darkened Jack's eyes.

"I don't know," she admitted, trading the grooming brush for a mane comb. "I don't have a death wish, but I don't have a lot of time left here. I just don't think I can leave without doing all I can to help stop this guy from killing again."

"I'll help you, if you want to do it." Jack's dark gaze met hers. "I know a guy with the paper in Jackson. I can set up an interview with him. He's a good guy—he won't take advantage. He'll agree to whatever precautions we think are necessary to keep you safe."

"Riley will be furious with you."

"I'm a big boy. Besides, I'm faster than he is. He'd have to catch me."

Hannah chuckled softly. "How quickly could you set it up?" Time was too short as it was.

"I can call him right now." Jack pulled his cell phone from his pocket. "You want to do it?"

She nibbled her lip, doubts creeping in now that the moment of decision was at hand. Was Riley's idea the better choice? Should she grab the next flight out of Wyoming and return home to the safety of her family, even if it meant turning her back on the best chance to catch Emily's killer that might ever come Riley's way?

The thought of Riley Patterson spending the rest of his life entrapped by his need for justice made the decision for her. "Let's do it," she said, meeting Jack's questioning eyes. "Call your friend."

"YOU'RE NOT SAYING YOU THINK she's right, are you?" Riley whipped around and gave his friend a look of disbelief.

"No, that's not what I'm saying." Joe held his hands up defensively. "At least, not exactly."

Riley slumped into the armchair, frustrated. If it were anyone but Hannah, would he be trying to stop her? On the merits, her idea was solid. The killer *was* getting bold—and therefore sloppy. There had probably never been a better time to take the offense against him.

But the thought of letting that bastard near Hannah, even if it made him a sitting duck, made his blood run cold.

Losing Emily had almost killed him. If Hannah died, too...

"How about a compromise?" Joe asked. "No making her a target—but she sticks around for the rest of her vacation."

"She's too easy to trace to me."

"So take her out of town. She wanted to see Grand Teton— I'll get Jim Tanner to book you a couple of rooms in Jackson Hole and you can do the tourist thing. Maybe she can relax a little, remember something new—"

"That just puts her closer to the killer's hunting grounds."

"Are you in love with her?"

Riley looked up sharply. "What kind of question is that?"

"It's not a crime to fall in love again." The gentleness in Joe's voice only made Riley angrier.

"Hannah Cooper is here only because I hoped she would remember something else about the attack on her," Riley said with a firmness he didn't feel. "I think she's remembered all she can, so it's time for her to go home."

"Good to know," Hannah said quietly from the doorway to the den. She met Riley's startled gaze with moist green eyes.

"Hannah—"

She turned and walked down the hall toward her room.

The look Joe gave Riley was as hard as a punch. "Who are you trying to impress with your loner act, Riley? Emily?" Joe stood and paced angrily to the doorway, turning to deliver one last shot. "Emily would hate what you're becoming." He walked out without another word.

Riley leaned forward in the armchair, resting his aching head in his hands. He hadn't cried since Emily's funeral, but hot tears gathered in his eyes right now, stinging painfully. He blinked them back, refusing to give in to the weakness. Anger, not grief, was what kept him upright these days. He couldn't afford to fall apart.

Not now, when he was closer than he'd ever been to finally catching the man who'd stolen the best part of his life.

"HE DIDN'T MEAN IT LIKE it sounded." Jack took the shirt out of Hannah's suitcase and put it back on the bed with the other shirts stacked there. "I've known him longer than you have. I know when he cares about someone. He cares about you."

She snatched the shirt back from the stack and shoved it into the suitcase. "I know he cares about me. But not enough to keep me here."

"Are you in love with him?"

She glared at Jack. "I'm not stupid."

"That's not an answer."

"Yes, it is." She punctuated the statement by slamming a pair of socks into the suitcase.

"It's not stupid to love someone."

She slumped to the bed. "It is if that someone is in love with someone else."

Jack cocked his head, his eyes narrowing. "We're not talking about Riley anymore, are we?"

"Not entirely," she admitted.

Jack leaned back on the bed, propping himself up with his elbows. "So tell Dr. Jack all about it."

She rolled her eyes at him, not wanting to be amused. But his humor was contagious, and her lips crooked slightly in response. "A week ago, this was all just a pitiful memory I was mostly over," she started. "I mean, it was four years ago, and it ended the way it was supposed to end—"

"With some other woman getting the guy?"

"He was always hers. She was his first love, and neither of them really got over it. I thought I loved him enough for both of us." She buried her face in her hands, mortified by the memory of her foolishness. "I was such an idiot."

"I've seen bigger idiots, trust me." Jack looked at her with sympathy. "How far did it get?"

She flushed with embarrassment. "The bachelor party."

Jack winced. "That far, huh?"

She lifted her chin, finding the steel at her center even though her heart was breaking a little. "I know Riley's not going to suddenly get over Emily just because he met me. I'm not going to fool myself into thinking otherwise. Does that answer your question?"

"No," he said with a smile. "But, that's not even the most important question anymore. Are you going back home?"

She shook her head. "I have three more days of vacation left, and I have an interview with a reporter."

"That's the spirit."

"But I am leaving here," she added, reaching for the stack of shirts again.

"I don't think you should."

"Riley's decided I should leave."

"I'm asking you to stay," he countered stubbornly. "You can stay as my guest."

"It's Riley's house."

"He'll cool down and see reason," Jack said confidently. "As long as you don't tell him about the press interview."

"You think I should lie to him?"

"I think you should just not tell him." Jack reached into the suitcase and started removing the clothing she'd already packed. "Mark Archibald's meeting us at Kent's Steakhouse at five. I'll tell Riley you need time to cool off and I'm taking you out for dinner. That's not a lie, right?"

Hannah had to smile a little at that, remembering how Riley had tried to keep the lies they were telling Jack as close to the truth as possible. They were more like brothers than either of them realized. "No, it's not a lie," she agreed. "We are going to dinner and I do need time to cool off."

And maybe, once the plan was in action, Riley would see why it was the only real choice she'd had.

THE INTERVIEW WITH THE reporter went as well as she could have hoped. Mark Archibald was friendly, funny and sympathetic. He asked good questions, which she answered as honestly as she could, while keeping a few of the details to herself, like the silver belt buckle and the fact that the killer had worn latex gloves when he attacked. She knew the police liked to keep some things back, in case they got a call from someone claiming to be the killer.

She made it clear, however, that there was more she remembered that she wasn't telling. She hoped Mark would make that fact just as clear in his article. She had to make herself as tempting to the killer as possible.

"It'll be in the paper tomorrow morning," Jack said on the drive back. He seemed jittery and energized, as if the cloak and dagger game they were playing had brought him to life. That definitely wasn't how Riley had reacted to lying, she remembered. Maybe he and Jack weren't so alike, after all.

"You need to calm down or Riley will know something's up," she suggested.

He grinned. "I know. I just—I think it's going to work. I think it's going to smoke this freak out and get a little justice for Em."

"And for the other women, too," Hannah added soberly.

His grin faded. "For the other women, too." He parked his truck next to Riley's in the yard. "I'm going to go feed the horses. You go on in."

"Coward," she said, but lightly, because it probably wasn't a good idea for Riley to see Jack as wound up as he was right now. Riley would wonder what his brother-in-law was up to.

She went into the house alone, not certain what she'd find. The kitchen was empty, though he'd left the light on over the sink so she wouldn't be entering into darkness. The hallway was dark, but a light shone in the guest room.

She entered her room to find Riley sitting on the bed, holding the sweater she'd left lying on her bed when she'd changed clothes for dinner with Jack and the reporter.

He looked up at her, his expression calm and regretful. "I didn't tell Joe the truth," he said.

She stopped at the rocking chair near the wood stove and sat, folding her hands on her lap. She held his gaze, waiting for him to elaborate. She wasn't sure what she wanted to hear from him—the blunt, harsh truth or some half-baked point-less apology. Either way, it was going to hurt.

"I'm not just using you to find Emily's murderer. I do care about whether or not you get hurt." He bent forward, his forearms resting on his knees. He looked as bone-weary as she felt. "The last three years have been hard."

"Sounds like an understatement," she murmured.

His pain-darkened eyes lifted to meet hers. "I used to be a very different man. I wasn't driven, I wasn't focused. I just enjoyed life as it came. Rode out whatever happened, not worrying too much about it. I had my health, I had my friends, I had Emily."

She didn't want to think about how much his description of his former life matched her own. Despite the broken heart she'd told Jack about, her life had been pretty good. Pretty easy. She'd done well in school, never having to struggle to achieve. Surrounded by a loving, happy family and the friends she'd grown up with, she'd gone to college just as planned, took a job at the Marina because it was what she'd always assumed she'd do.

What in her life had ever been a struggle before now?

"I sometimes think Joe just sticks around out of stubbornness. I'm a terrible friend to him. He and Jane were in a dangerous mess a couple of years ago, and I barely managed to pull my head out of my backside enough to give them a hand right about the time it was all over." He looked away, his face flushed with shame. "My other friends gave up a long time ago. I keep telling my parents I'm fine, but they know. They just don't know what to do about it."

"It's hard to know what to say to someone who's hurting," she said, thinking about her brother J.D., who was, at least, lucky enough to have his two kids to keep him putting one foot in front of the other every day.

"It's not their fault. It's mine." He briefly pressed his palms against his temples, then dropped his hands to his knees. "I've pushed people away because it took all the energy I had to keep going, keep focusing on finding out who killed Emily and those other women. I can't—I can't let other things matter."

His voice faltered, the words trembling on his tongue. She wanted to go to him, pull him into her arms and share the burden, but he clearly wasn't ready for that.

Might never be ready.

"But you matter," he said finally, so softly that she almost missed it. He looked up at her, his eyes blazing blue fire. "You matter."

He lurched off the bed, towering over her for a long, breathless moment, then bent and put his hands on the rocking chair arms, leaning close enough that she felt his breath warm on her cheeks. "You can't put yourself at any further risk. Do you understand? If something happened to you—"

Tears burned her eyes and spilled down her cheeks as he pulled her to her feet and into his embrace. His mouth descended on hers, fiery sweet and urgent. She wrapped her arms around his neck, pulling him closer, needing the heat of him against her trembling body. Guilt mingled with desire as she struggled to find the center of her suddenly upended world.

He edged her toward the bed, turning and falling until she lay beneath him, her back against the mattress. He drew back long enough to cradle her head between his hands and gaze down at her with a question in his eyes.

Her body screamed for him to keep touching her, keep kissing her, to fill the aching, empty places inside her. But her mind was dark with regret, because she'd already set into motion something that would put her in much more danger, the one thing he'd just begged her not to do.

"Stop," she said softly as he bent to kiss her again.

Riley went still, gazing at her with suddenly wary eyes. She felt the rapid drumbeat of his heart against her chest.

"I talked to a reporter tonight," she confessed.

Chapter Twelve

Riley froze, Hannah's admission washing over him like ice water. His arms trembled as he hovered over her, trying to process what he'd just heard.

"I told him some of what happened to me." The words spilled from Hannah's lips in an inflectionless rush. "I held back most of the details—the belt buckle, the latex gloves. But I mentioned that my attacker posed as a cop. And I made it clear that I remembered more than I was telling the reporter."

He rolled away from her, sitting up with his back to her. Cold, hard fear settled in his gut as a dozen terrifying outcomes rattled through his brain like a horrible slide show.

What had she done?

"I'm sorry," she said, regret threaded through her voice. "I thought I had to do something to push things forward. I have so little time left before I have to go back home."

If she even made it home alive, he thought bleakly. "You shouldn't have done that." His voice came out hard and strangled.

She didn't answer.

"How did you get in touch with a reporter?"

She couldn't answer that question without implicating

Jack. She hedged instead. "Does it matter? It was my choice to do it."

He looked inclined to probe deeper, but to her relief, he just sighed and asked, "Can we stop it?"

"No. He was writing and filing the story as soon as he got back to the office. It's probably already on the press."

He pushed to his feet, not ready to give up. He pulled out his cell phone. "Who was the reporter?"

"I don't even remember the paper—it's a daily out of Jackson. The reporter's name is Mark Archibald." She caught his arm, tugging him around to look at her. "I don't think we should stop it, Riley."

Her chin was up, her jaw squared. A sinking feeling settled in his gut, and he shook off her hand. "Like hell." He flipped open the phone and dialed the number for Teton County Sheriff Jim Tanner.

Tanner answered on the second ring. "Jim Tanner."

"Sheriff Tanner, it's Riley Patterson." Not waiting for the chief's response, he tersely outlined what Hannah had told him about her meeting with the Jackson reporter. "Can you get the story killed?"

After a brief pause, Jim Tanner answered, "No."

"Why the hell not?"

"The First Amendment comes to mind," Tanner answered in a dry drawl. "Also, we're doing a disservice to the communities we serve by holding back on this any longer."

Riley couldn't believe what he was hearing. "This article will put Hannah Cooper's life in greater danger."

"And not running it will put the lives of women all over Wyoming in greater danger," Tanner countered firmly. "Hannah Cooper has a cop playing bodyguard for her twenty-four hours a day. Those other women don't even know the flashing blue light in their rearview mirrors could mean their lives are over."

Riley slumped against the bedroom wall, reason starting to gain on the galloping fear eating away at his insides. They'd only sat on the story this long to give Hannah time to remember more before they went public. But the women of Wyoming were sitting ducks with no idea what might be lurking out there to snuff out their lives. They didn't know what to look for or how to protect themselves.

He closed his eyes. "Okay. It runs."

He heard Hannah release a slow, shaky breath. Opening his eyes, he found her watching him with eyes bright with tears.

"I should probably schedule a press conference once the story breaks," Tanner added, a hint of weary resignation tinting his voice. "Want to be part of it?"

"Hold on a sec." Riley covered the mouthpiece. "Is the reporter going to say anything about where you're staying?" he asked Hannah.

"No," she answered. "The idea for this story was to get the killer's attention and get him thinking about me again, instead of going on the hunt for another woman."

He saw the fear lurking like a vulture behind her eyes, but the brave determination in her voice inspired his admiration. He might be mad as hell that she'd put her life on the line, but he had gained a new respect for her courage.

"Keep me out of it," he told Tanner. Having him there might provide the killer with a clue where to look for Hannah.

"Okay," Tanner agreed. "I'll see if I can get an early look at what the paper's going to run with. If I can, want me to fax you a copy?"

"Fax it to the police department." He gave Jim Tanner the station's fax number. "Joe will get it to me."

He rang off, shoving his phone in his pocket. "Tanner thinks it should run," he told Hannah.

"What do you think?" she asked.

He released a long, slow breath, trying to answer with his head instead of his gut. "I think the women of Wyoming should know there's someone out there pretending to be a cop, pulling them over, abducting and killing them."

The corners of her lip twitched briefly, though the relief didn't quite make it to her eyes. "I'm sorry I blindsided you with it."

"I'd have been more blindsided if I'd opened the paper in the morning and found you on page one," he admitted. "I appreciate the heads-up."

Uncertainty flitted across her face, but he didn't know how to reassure her. He wasn't sure he even wanted to. The danger surrounding her was about to grow exponentially thanks to one small newspaper story, and he found himself wanting to retreat, to save himself from the torment he knew might be coming.

What if he couldn't keep her safe?

He was already half a man, thanks to losing Emily. If something happened to Hannah, would there be anything left?

"I need to go lock up for the night. We'll talk in the morning." He rose to go.

Behind him, he heard her take a quick breath, as if she had something to say. But he didn't turn back to look at her, and she didn't speak, so he closed the door behind him and went out to wait for Jack.

THE WOMAN STARING AT HANNAH in the mirror looked like crap. Purple shadows bruised the skin beneath her eyes, dark against her pale cheeks. Her body still buzzed with unsatisfied hunger, but her heart felt as hard and cold as a rock.

Riley had left the bedroom only moments ago, but he'd distanced himself from her long before he closed the door. She'd watched it happen, saw his expression shutter and the light in his eyes blink out.

He'd had too much pain in his life already. And she'd just asked him to take a chance on a whole lot more.

No wonder he'd walked away.

It was bittersweet, knowing that Riley really did care about her. Maybe not enough to build a relationship on, but she supposed it was something she could take home with her, like a secret souvenir, to bring out now and then to remember what it was like to be wrapped up tight in Riley's arms.

But would that be enough? Could she go home, never to return, and be content with nothing but a memory?

WHEN JACK CAME BACK FROM the stable, Riley was waiting for him. Jack didn't even have time to say hello before Riley pushed him against the door.

"You went behind my back and called a reporter in."

Jack's expression went from puzzled to guilty. "Hannah told you."

"No, but *you* should have."

He sighed. "I'm sorry. But someone needed to do something, and you were about to pack Hannah off to Alabama rather than listen to what she was trying to tell you. She *wanted* to talk to Mark."

"Because she feels guilty about being the one who got away. You know how that feels, Jack."

Jack blanched, and Riley felt a little ashamed of himself. But it was the truth, however harsh. One of the things that tied him and Jack together, now that Emily was gone, was good old-fashioned guilt.

He was a cop, Jack was a rodeo cowboy. They were the

ones with dangerous lives, not Emily, who'd been the nurturer. The healer. And yet, she'd been the one to go too early. Either one of them would have traded places with her in a heartbeat.

Jack gave Riley a little push out of his way. "I know something else, Riley. I know what it feels like to need to make things right." He crossed to the kitchen sink, fiddled with the cups drying on the rack, and finally just rested his hands on the counter, his head dropping to his chest. "Hannah's time here is almost over, and she feels she hasn't done anything to get you any closer to catching that bastard. It's been eating her up."

"You think I didn't notice?" Riley challenged, growing angrier by the second.

Jack turned slowly to look at him. "Did you? Sometimes I think the only thing you see these days is your own pain."

Riley flexed his fingers, longing to drive his fist into the stubborn set of Jack's square jaw. He forced himself to stay where he was, needing distance to get a grip on himself.

"It's not me you're angry at," Jack added.

"Wrong," Riley snapped. "It's not just that you set up the meeting, though that's bad enough. It's that you didn't have the guts to be a man and tell me about it."

"You would have stopped it."

"That's an excuse for lying?"

"I did what I thought I had to do," Jack answered. "For Hannah—and for Emily."

A thread of dark pain turned Riley's anger into weary resignation. "I trusted you with Hannah's safety and you put her in danger. How am I supposed to trust you after that?"

Jack looked as if Riley had slapped him. "I guess you can't." He turned on his heel and headed out of the kitchen.

Riley followed him into the den. "I have enough to deal with, just keeping Hannah safe, and what the two of you did is only going to make things harder." He realized Jack was starting to pack his bag. "Going somewhere?"

"I don't stay where I'm not wanted."

Riley sighed. "Where would you go?"

Jack glared at him over his shoulder. "I didn't come here to mooch. I came here because this was Emily's home. I have enough money to rent a motel room for a few days."

"Then what?"

"That's my business." Jack stuffed the last pair of jeans into his bag and started past Riley.

"Jack—" Riley went after him, catching his arm at the door. Down the hallway, the door to Hannah's room opened, and she stepped halfway into the hall, her eyes meeting his.

"Is something wrong?" she asked.

Jack set his bag on the floor and walked toward her. "I'm heading out."

Hannah looked down at the bag, her brow wrinkling with dismay. "You're leaving?"

"Just like a tumbleweed, sweetheart." Jack patted her cheek. "It's been great meeting you, Hannah Cooper. If I'm ever in Alabama, I'll look you up."

Hannah followed him into the kitchen, with Riley on her heels. "What's going on?"

"Riley's had his fill of me, I think."

"That's not what I said," Riley insisted.

"If this is about the reporter, that was my doing, Riley!" Hannah grabbed his arm, desperation in her eyes. "Jack did what I asked him to do. Please—"

"I didn't tell him to leave," he said weakly.

"Did you tell him to stay?" she countered, her eyes flashing with fire. "If anyone leaves, it should be me. It was my idea. I'm the outsider."

"Stop it, Hannah." Jack put his hand on her shoulder. "It's time. This just gives me an excuse to make a dramatic exit." When he looked up at Riley, his dark eyes were warm with understanding. "I'm just hiding out here anyway because I don't want to face what I left behind in Texas."

If Riley knew his brother-in-law at all, what he left behind in Texas was a broken heart.

"I need to see if I can fix what I broke," Jack added softly.

That was a first, Riley thought. Maybe the kid really had started to grow up this time.

"I'm not kicking you out," he said aloud, not because he thought it would soften the resolve he saw in Jack's eyes, but because it needed to be said.

"I know." As Hannah stepped aside, Jack stepped forward and held out his hand.

Riley took it, giving it a firm, warm shake. "At least stay the night. Where are you going to find a motel that'll take you in this time of night?

"You'd be surprised." Jack grinned wryly. "But don't worry—I ran into an old friend yesterday while I was out. He said I could come visit whenever, so I'm taking him up on it."

"Need any money?"

Jack laughed softly. "No, but thanks for offering."

Riley glanced at Hannah, who still looked upset. He wished he could reassure her that everything was okay, but it would take forever to try to explain the complexities of his relationship with his brother-in-law. He settled for an apologetic smile and put his hand on Jack's shoulder. "I'll walk you out."

Hannah remained inside as they walked out to where Jack's truck was parked. Jack tossed the bag into the passenger seat and turned to Riley. "Take care of yourself, man."

Riley pulled Jack into a hug. "You, too. I hope you can fix whatever you left broken down in Texas."

"I hope you can fix what you've broken here." Jack stepped back and gave Riley a smile. "You've got three more days, man. She could change your life."

Jack climbed into the truck, shut the door and cranked the engine. He gave a short wave as he backed down the gravel drive, then he was gone.

Riley walked slowly back to the house, Jack's parting words still ringing in his ears. *She could change your life.*

That was the problem wasn't it? His life had already changed, irrevocably. Since Emily's death, it had become twenty-four hours a day, seven days a week of trying to cope with a world that no longer made any sense.

Yes, Hannah Cooper had been the first person in three years who'd broken through that haze and made him feel something good again. But how much of that was just two young, healthy bodies doing what young, healthy bodies do? How much of what he felt for her was wrapped up in the fact that she was his best break in the case that had haunted him for three years?

She deserved more. She deserved better.

And yet, when he found her waiting there in the kitchen for his return, her green eyes sympathetic, it took all the control he had not to sweep her into his arms and carry her into the nearest bedroom.

"It wasn't his fault."

Riley crossed to the refrigerator and opened it, though he wasn't the least bit hungry. Anything to drag his gaze away from Hannah. "Jack and I are okay. I promise."

"Then why'd he leave?"

"Because I think he realized staying here was just an

excuse to hide from his problems." Riley closed the refrigerator, empty-handed.

He supposed the same thing could be said about his own life for the last three years. God knew, he'd buried himself in this investigation as an escape from his own pain, though he couldn't really say he'd been successful.

"I've been hiding here, hiding behind you, for too long," Hannah said. "I have three days left of my vacation, and what have I been doing? I haven't remembered anything new since the belt buckle. I haven't even really tried." She slammed her hand against the table, the sudden sound putting his nerves on hard alert. "I have to do something, Riley."

"You already have," he said, knowing it wasn't going to appease her.

The look she gave him proved him right. "I think I need to do more interviews. Maybe play up the tourist in jeopardy angle. It would get plenty of play, wouldn't it?"

"And draw the killer right to you." The thought made his stomach hurt.

She crossed to stand in front of him, her eyes shining with a manic light. "Exactly."

He shook his head. "No way in hell."

"We could come up with a way to lure him in. Police would be everywhere. I'd be safe."

Everything inside him rebelled. "Hannah, that's crazy. You're letting your frustrations overcome your good sense."

"You're letting your fears overcome your cop instincts," she countered passionately. "If it was you, you'd do it."

"That's different."

"Because I'm a woman?"

"Because I can't—" He bit off the rest of the thought, not ready to say it aloud. Not even to himself.

She took his hand and threaded her fingers through his, gazing up at him with a warm, soft gaze. "Why don't we do this? Let's table the discussion for tonight. We can wait and see how things go tomorrow when the article comes out."

"Okay." He grabbed the reprieve, weary of arguing with her when all he really wanted to do was hold her close, to bury himself in her soft warmth and make the hard, dark world outside the two of them disappear.

"Let's just have a nice, quiet evening, okay?" She tugged his hand, pulling him down the hall to the den. She let go long enough to drop on to the sofa and pat the cushion beside her. "Let's see if we can find a movie on TV. Something funny."

He handed her the remote, content to let her choose. She found something old, in black and white. Cary Grant, Katharine Hepburn and a leopard. He paid little attention to the story, content to listen to Hannah's peals of laughter and the feel of her warm and solid beside him.

Three more days alone in this house with Hannah was a lifetime.

And not nearly long enough.

THE ARTICLE IN THE JACKSON paper was exactly what Hannah had hoped for, although she could tell from the grim look on Riley's face that he thought she'd gone too far.

"Look at it this way," she said as they walked down to the stable after breakfast, "if it grabs the killer's attention, then maybe he won't be out hunting for another woman to kill just to prove a point to us."

"Yeah, he'll just be looking to kill you."

"And you'll be there to stop him," she said firmly, refusing to allow the little knot of terror tap dancing in her belly to win the battle.

"It doesn't always work that way." The stricken tone of Riley's voice caught her by surprise.

"I know," she relented, stopping halfway to the stable to take his hand. He turned to look at her, his eyes shadowy beneath the brim of his hat.

"I've been after this guy for three years. God knows how many more years he's been killing women that we don't even know about." Riley's fingers tightened around hers. "I couldn't stop him from killing those other women." His voice grew a notch fainter. "I didn't stop him from killing Emily."

"How were you supposed to do that?" Hannah asked, torn between wanting to hug him and wanting to shake him. "Drive her to work every day? God, Riley, you sound just like that guy at the gas station!"

Riley's brow wrinkled. "What guy at the gas station?"

Hannah blinked, surprised by the question, until she realized she'd never mentioned the man she'd run into at the gas station on Highway 287. In fact, until this moment, she hadn't remembered him at all. "He was at the other pump—at that station on 287. He was filling up his car, and he saw the rental-car plate. Said I was brave to drive around all by myself in a strange place. Only, I could tell he really meant I was stupid to be traveling alone."

"Did he say anything else?"

She shook her head. "I don't think so. He finished by then and drove off."

"Did you get a good look at him?"

"Not really—there was a pump between us, and he had a hat on, and sunglasses." She frowned. "You think he might be the guy who pulled me over?"

"I don't know. Was he in a car or a truck?"

"A car." It had been a dark sedan, but beyond that, she

couldn't really remember anything. "I guess it could have been the same car. I really don't remember much but the flashing blue light, to be honest."

He laid his palm against her cheek. "It's something new. Joe's got someone going through the receipts from the gas station. If he paid with a credit or debit card, we'll know who he is soon." He dropped his hand and headed for the stable.

She followed, her mind reeling. Had she actually spoken to the killer that day at the gas station?

Had that one simple exchange marked her for death?

Chapter Thirteen

"We found Hannah's credit-card receipt from the Lassiter station, and a few others sprinkled through the day, but nothing right around the same time." Joe Garrison gave Riley an apologetic look. "Guy must've paid cash."

"Damn it," Riley growled, slanting a look at Hannah, who sat in one of the armchairs in front of Joe's desk. She'd been so hopeful on the drive into town, but now she looked as if Joe had kicked her right in the teeth.

"What if it was him?" she asked faintly. "I can't even tell you what color hair he had, or what shape his face was. Why didn't I pay more attention?"

"Because you weren't expecting some nosy guy at the gas station to track you and try to kill you," Joe said sensibly.

"And we don't even know if it's the same guy," Riley added, laying his hand on her shoulder. He soothed her tense muscles beneath his palm and turned back to Joe. "Has Jim Tanner held his press conference yet?"

Joe glanced at the wall clock. "It's supposed to start in about twenty minutes."

More waiting, Riley thought. Hannah's growing impatience was contagious.

"What about security video?" Hannah asked suddenly. "Don't most places like that have cameras trained on the gas islands to discourage gas theft?"

"The Lassiter station's security video hasn't worked in over a year," Joe answered. "Population is so low in Wyoming, people here don't take the same precautions you find in other states. It's just not a big problem, most of the time."

"I bet he knew it, too," Hannah said glumly. "This guy seems to be a step or two ahead of us."

"He's clearly a local," Riley agreed.

"He wore gloves, so no fingerprints. He moved fast before I even got a look at his face, so I can't ID him. Even at the gas station, I never got a good look at him. Now that I think about it, he was careful not to turn his face toward me." She looked up at Riley. "Maybe he was already in hunting mode."

It was possible, he conceded. "Did anybody find out who was working that shift at the Lassiter station? Maybe he'd remember if our guy hung around longer than usual."

"We've got the cashier's name. I have Prentiss tracking the guy down to see if he remembers anything from the day of the attack." Joe picked up the television remote and hit the power button. The small television on the credenza near the window flickered on, the volume low.

No press conference yet, just a syndicated talk show, Riley noted. He turned back to look at Hannah. Her green eyes met his, shining with a mix of excitement and dread.

He knew just how she felt. He'd never been as close to finding the killer as he was now, yet he wasn't sure he was really prepared for the uncertainty that lay ahead. What if, despite all efforts to keep her safe, Hannah ended up hurt— or worse? How could he live with such an outcome?

And what if they actually found her attacker, and it turned

out Emily hadn't been one of his victims after all? Could he start from scratch, devoting more years of his life to nothing but cold, comfortless vengeance?

"Here we go," Joe said suddenly, and he turned up the volume on the TV.

As Sheriff Tanner laid out the basic details of the pepper-spray attack, Riley found his gaze drawn to Hannah. Emotions played across her face as she listened, a battle of fear and hope. As much as he had riding on this case, she had more. It was her life in danger, and she'd stayed here to help in spite of that fact, when a lot of other people would have gone home.

She was one hell of a woman.

I'm going to keep you safe, sweetheart, he vowed silently. *Whatever it takes.*

On television, Tanner had finished his statement and was taking questions. Most were utterly predictable. Did they have a suspect? Were other women at risk? Was Ms. Cooper going to make herself available for questions?

"What is he going to say when they ask if there's a connection to the murder in Grand Teton State Park?" Riley asked Joe, knowing the question was coming.

Before Joe could answer, a reporter asked just that question. Joe nodded toward the television.

"We aren't certain, but we're proceeding as if there's a possibility," Tanner answered carefully. "That's why it's important for women traveling alone to be especially careful. Local and state agencies have agreed that no law-enforcement officer driving an unmarked vehicle will attempt a traffic stop in Wyoming. So if such a vehicle attempts to pull you over, do not stop. Call nine-one-one and drive to a public place. Do not stop in an isolated place for any reason."

"What if you have car trouble?"

"Lock your doors, call for help if you have a phone. I know cell service doesn't work in all areas, but the people of Wyoming are friendly, helpful people. The Wyoming Department of Safety and several corporate partners are making distress signs available for motorists. These can be placed in windows to alert other drivers to your need for assistance."

He motioned to his right and a uniformed officer brought out a long banner with the words "Assistance Needed—Call 911" printed in block letters across the length.

"Please remember—if you see this sign, it is not a good idea to stop and give aid yourself. Please contact the local authorities and alert us to the problem."

"They're afraid the killer might use this to lure in unsuspecting good Samaritans," Hannah murmured.

"It's possible," Riley agreed.

The rest of the questions were little more than rewording of previous questions. Tanner put an end to the questions and left the stage, and the station returned to the local news anchors in the studio.

Joe turned off the television and looked at Riley. "That went okay, don't you think?"

It could have been a lot worse, Riley had to concede. God knew he was relieved to have information about the killer in front of the public.

Joe's phone buzzed. "Boss?" Over the intercom came the tinny voice of Bill Handley, the day-shift desk sergeant. "Sheriff Tanner from the Teton County Sheriff's Department on line one."

Joe exchanged a quick look with Riley and picked up the phone. "Garrison." He listened a moment, glancing at Hannah. "Yes, they're both here. I'm putting you on speakerphone."

He pushed a button and Jim Tanner's voice came over the line. "Good morning, Patterson. Ms. Cooper."

"Hello, Sheriff Tanner," Hannah murmured.

"Tanner," Riley added gruffly, his stomach knotting up.

"I'm just going to get straight to the point," Tanner said. "I have an idea to go on the offense on this case, but it requires your help, Ms. Cooper."

"No," Riley said firmly.

Both Joe and Hannah looked up at him, startled.

"What do you have in mind, Sheriff?" Hannah asked.

"I want you to give an interview to one of the TV stations and let them know that you're seeing a psychiatrist here at the hospital in Jackson—someone who's helping you recover some of the memories you lost thanks to the concussion."

"You want to set her up as bait," Riley interpreted.

"In a controlled way. I have already discussed the idea with one of the hospital's staff psychiatrists, and she's willing to go along with the plan."

"I'll do it," Hannah said swiftly.

"No, she won't," Riley said, glaring back at her when she once again turned angry eyes toward him.

"When do you want me in Jackson?" Hannah asked, her gaze doing fierce battle with Riley's.

"I need time to set things up, but I think we'll want to shoot for the local evening newscast," Tanner answered. "Give them a day to promo the interview, make sure our guy knows to watch. So, if you could be in Jackson tomorrow morning, we can get the ball rolling."

"Set it up," Hannah said firmly.

"Hannah, no," Riley pleaded softly. "It's too dangerous."

"Call Chief Garrison when it's set," she added, her eyes softening. "He'll pass the information along to me."

"Thank you, Ms. Cooper. You're doing a brave thing." Admiration rang in Tanner's voice.

"I just want this man caught," Hannah replied.

Tanner rang off and Joe hung up the phone. He looked at Riley, sympathy in his eyes, then spoke to Hannah. "If you want to back out at any point, don't feel obligated to go through with this plan. I know Sheriff Tanner will do all he can to keep you safe, and I'll make sure I'm in on things, too, but nobody can promise you that there's no danger."

"I'm not trying to be a hero," Hannah said. "I want to be able to go back home and sleep at night knowing I didn't chicken out on a chance to catch a really bad guy who's hurt a lot of people." The look she gave Riley made his heart hurt.

"If you're doing this for me—"

"For you, for me, for that woman in the national park and all those other women you told me about." She leaned over and took his hand. "For Emily."

He lifted her hand, pressed his lips against her knuckles. The arguments he wanted to make died in his throat.

Joe cleared his throat. "I guess that's it for now."

Riley didn't let go of Hannah's hand as he turned to look at his friend. "I want you in on everything. Every bit of the planning. Can you stay on Tanner, make sure he's covering all the possibilities?"

"Of course. But don't you want to do that yourself?"

Riley looked at Hannah again. "No, I'm going to spend the next twenty-four hours talking her out of this crazy idea."

So, SHE WAS REMEMBERING, he thought, replaying the sheriff's press conference in his head.

Jim Tanner hadn't said it in so many words, but clearly he was holding something back, something that put that smug half smile on his face throughout the entire press conference.

So far, he hadn't had much luck finding out where the girl was hiding out. His friend at the Sheriff's Department didn't know. He'd even made a point of running into Mark Archibald, the reporter who'd managed the first interview with Hannah Cooper, but he wasn't dropping any clues about the woman's whereabouts.

No need to panic yet. Whatever the woman remembered, it wasn't enough to implicate him. She'd never gotten a good look at him; he'd been careful, wearing nondescript clothing and his hat low over his face. She might have seen his belt buckle, but that wouldn't hurt him. He wore it only when he was hunting, and it had been a hand-me-down, not a purchase.

Still, he'd feel better when he finally tracked her down.

HANNAH COCKED HER HEAD, watching Riley flip the steak on the grill. He looked over his shoulder and smiled at her, fueling her suspicion that he was playing some sort of game with her. On the up side, at least she was getting a steak dinner out of it. But she couldn't help wondering why he wasn't trying to talk her out of playing bait for the killer.

Driving home from the Canyon Creek Police station, he hadn't said a word about Sheriff Tanner's plan. On the contrary, he'd taken the scenic route, detouring along lightly traveled side roads winding through open range, where horses and cattle grazed on the last good grass before winter arrived. He was a charming tour guide, telling her all about the local legends from a time when cowboys were kings.

"Just north of here," he had told her, "lies the Wind River Indian Reservation. Northern Arapaho and Eastern Shoshone. Emily's mother grew up there."

Which explained Jack's coloring.

"Emily's mother died when she was little—not long after Jack was born. They grew up with their dad, so they never really knew much about their mother's side of the family. She always regretted that." Riley's voice had gone faint, as it often did when he spoke of his late wife.

He'd changed the subject, and the conversation for the rest of the ride home had been light and inconsequential.

Certainly no mention of Sheriff Tanner's plan to put her in the killer's crosshairs.

"Are you sure I can't help you with something?"

"Got it covered," he assured her. He closed the grill cover and came to sit next to her on the rough, wooden bench set against the back wall of the house. He edged closer, enfolding her cold hands in his. "Are you sure you want to wait out here with me? Your hands are like icicles."

She leaned against him, happy for his body heat. Though the house blocked some of the wind whipping down from the north, the sun was already beginning to set, robbing her of its waning warmth. "And miss watching you play chef? Not a chance."

He wrapped his arm around her, pulling her closer. "Better?"

He smelled like wood smoke and grilling steak. Her stomach growled, and she chuckled inwardly. Tasty, indeed.

"Somebody's hungry." His low, growly baritone rumbled in her ear, turning the statement into a nerve-melting double entendre. She looked up to find him watching her, his gaze restless.

She swallowed hard, her heart fluttering wildly. "Yes."

He bent his head to nuzzle the side of her neck. His lips traced a shivery path up to her ear. "Me, too."

So, this is what he's up to.

Resistance was impossible, even though she was onto his plan of distraction. By the time his mouth slid over the curve of her jaw, she was far beyond protest.

His lips found hers, moving lazily. She lifted her hands to his head, his crisp, short-cropped hair rasping against her palms, making them tingle. She pulled him closer, ready for the next course, but he gave her only a quick taste, his tongue brushing lightly over hers, before he pulled back. The kiss was an appetizer, only whetting her hunger.

"Don't want to burn anything," he murmured, pulling away and returning to the grill.

He grabbed a set of tongs and flipped the steaks. The smell wafting toward her made her mouth water.

At least she told herself it was the smell.

"You haven't given up on talking me out of the plan, have you?" she asked.

He glanced over his shoulder at her. "Did you think I would?"

She shook her head slowly. "It's not going to do you any good. You can't wine and dine me out of this."

He smiled slightly, his eyes dark with determination. "I wasn't expecting food to change your mind."

Oh, my. The unspoken promise of that statement sank in, spreading heat over her throat and down her back. The fleece coat she wore to fend against the evening chill felt suddenly heavy and constricting.

"And I'm out of wine," he added. "Afraid we'll have to go into this sober."

She unzipped her jacket, grateful for the cool rush of air. "I don't like wine anyway. Makes me sleepy."

"Exactly." He turned back to the grill.

Warning bells rang frantically in her brain, but walking away seemed beyond her. Instead, she scrambled mentally for a safe topic to cool down the heat rising between them. "I called my parents earlier. I told them what I had decided to do."

He looked over his shoulder again. "What did they say?"

"Not to do it, of course."

"Mom and Dad know best."

She pressed her lips into a tight line. "If they were in my position, they'd do what I'm doing. Where do you think I learned it from?"

His answer was to flip the peppers charring on the grill.

"I just hope they don't call my brothers and let them know what's up. I'm surprised Aaron hasn't called me already. He's the cop," she reminded him. "Chickasaw County's finest."

He closed the top of the grill again and turned around to look at her. "What would Aaron the cop tell you?"

"Not to do it," she answered.

"Seems to be the consensus." He walked slowly toward her, every step a seduction, whether he intended it to be so or not. She tried to look away, but her muscles seemed paralyzed.

A fly in a spider's web, she thought faintly. Then he sat beside her again, lifting one hand to cup her cheek. What was left of her rational side curled up and whimpered.

He had large hands, rough with work. He ran the pad of his thumb lightly across her bottom lip. "You have a beautiful mouth. Has anyone ever told you that?"

The memory his words evoked helped her gather up what was left of her self-control. "Yes."

His thumb stopped moving. "Whoever he was, he was right."

"He liked kissing me." She forced the words from her mouth, not because she wanted to talk about that painful time in her life, but because it was her best defense against Riley's potent seduction. "But he loved someone else."

Riley dropped his hand to his lap. "What happened?"

"He married her, not me."

Riley breathed deeply, bending forward to rest his forearms on his knees. "When was that?"

"About four years ago." She hadn't planned to tell him more, but the gentle encouragement in his eyes made her open up about Craig, their whirlwind romance, the wedding plans and the terrible moment when, at the bachelor's party, he confessed to Hannah's brother Aaron that he was still in love with another woman. "Aaron made him tell me the truth." She smiled wryly. "Craig's lucky. Aaron was really ticked."

Riley took it all in silently, his expression solemn. Surely he couldn't miss the parallels between then and now, between Craig's lingering feelings for his old flame and Riley's unending passion for his dead wife.

"I think I knew long before he told me." Shame burned the back of her neck. "I just thought I could change his mind. But you can't will a man to get over the woman he loves."

"No." Riley moved restlessly away from her and opened the top of the grill. The smell of grilled peppers and steak filled the light breeze, but she'd lost her appetite.

Apparently, he had as well. Turning off the grill, he transferred the meat and peppers to a couple of plates, but he returned to her side without bringing the food. He turned toward her on the bench, reaching out to take her chin in his hand. He lifted her face, making her look up at him.

The intensity of his gaze made her stomach tighten into a hot, tight knot. "I don't want you to go to Jackson tomorrow."

"I know."

"I don't know how to stop you. You've already said wining and dining won't work."

She had to laugh at that, and his lips curved in response, but he soon grew serious again.

"I can only tell you that I came damned near losing my mind when Emily died. I don't think I've gotten all of it back yet." He cradled her face with gentle strength. "If something happened to you, I don't think there'd be anything left of me."

Tears trembled on her lashes and tumbled down her cheeks. She blinked them back, fighting for control. "You hardly know me," she said, trying to be reasonable. But even as she spoke the words, she knew they were inadequate. In a few, brief days, she'd shared more about herself with him than she'd shared with most of her family. He knew the fears that hid behind her bravado, the longing she buried beneath her outward contentment.

He didn't have to contradict her. She saw in his eyes that he knew the complexity of their relationship went far beyond a few days of acquaintance. *Soul mates,* her traitorous mind whispered, and she couldn't disagree. But the truth didn't make Riley any less in love with his dead wife.

She closed her eyes and drew away from him, needing breathing room to gather the scraps of reason still left in her rattled brain and try to figure out what to do.

She wanted him. She couldn't have denied that truth if her life depended on it. And she also knew the futility of letting her desire become anything more demanding. They might have a deep and special connection, but that was no guarantee of happily ever after.

Could she settle for happily right now?

"Please don't go to Jackson tomorrow," he said.

She forced her eyes open, letting the tiny flicker of anger licking at her belly grow into a slow burn. "I told you my decision," she snapped. "You're going to have to respect it."

She stood and entered the house, leaning against the door for a second to calm her jangled nerves. She listened through the door for any sign that he intended to follow, but all she heard was the clatter of plates and cutlery.

A sudden crash made her jump, and she peeked through the small window set in the top of the door and saw Riley crouching by the grill, piling up pieces of a broken plate with swift, jerky movements.

She went to the guest room, closing the door behind her, and sat on the bed, hating herself for breaking the peace between them. He'd just opened up to her, sharing feelings she suspected he hadn't shared with anyone since Emily's death, and she'd rewarded him with a temper tantrum.

Nice, Hannah. Way to make sure the rest of your time in Wyoming is a living hell.

RILEY TOSSED THE PIECES of broken plate into a trash bag one by one, grimly enjoying the sound of each thunk. As irritated as he was at the moment, he found a strange sort of pleasure in the feeling. It had been a while since anyone had inspired in him a powerful emotion outside of grief.

He understood her frustration with his stubborn insistence that she back out of Jim Tanner's plan, but what choice did he have? He'd sacrificed a normal life in his quest to find Emily's killer, but he wasn't going to sacrifice Hannah.

Which was also a new sensation—caring about someone more than he cared about revenge.

He set the trash bag in the bin by the door and went back to the grill to gather up the food and take it inside.

Hannah was nowhere to be found. He glanced down the hall and saw the door to her room closed.

So she was hiding. Trying to stay mad? He knew she wasn't as angry at him as she wanted to be. But anger was better than vulnerability. He knew that better than most people.

He found a pair of clean plates and split the steaks and peppers between them. Going back to the drawer for flatware, he glanced down the hallway again. The door was still closed.

He waited until after he'd poured ice water in two glasses before he went down the hall to knock on the door. "Hannah?"

She didn't answer, but he could sense her listening just behind the door.

"If you don't answer me, I'm going to assume something bad happened to you and bust the door down," he warned.

The door opened and she stood on the other side, looking up at him with flashing green eyes. He took a step forward before he could stop himself.

She put her hands up, almost defensively, but when her fingers touched his chest, they curled into the fabric of his shirt, pulling him closer.

His heart rate soared as their bodies made contact. He couldn't have stopped his physical response if he'd wanted to.

She rose to her toes and pulled his head down, slanting her head back and fitting her mouth against his. He drank in her sweetness, fire building low and slow in his belly.

"I don't want to fight," she whispered, sliding her lips across the edge of his jaw.

He felt himself falling into her, the last shred of resistance gone. Pushing her back toward the bed, he fell atop her, shifting so that her body cradled his. Her thighs parting to welcome him, she tugged urgently at his shirt, her eyes glazed with hunger.

"Hannah—" he began, needing to be sure she knew what was about to happen between them, but she silenced him with her mouth, drawing him down to her with strong, determined arms.

There was nothing he could do but follow her into the sweet, desperate madness.

Chapter Fourteen

She rose beneath him, her strong fingers digging into the muscles of his back. The sound of her whispered endearments seemed as familiar as his own voice. Her body opened to him, soft and furnace hot, drawing him into a web of pure pleasure that left his body weak but his soul as strong and enduring as the Wyoming mountains. She clung to him, raining kisses over his cheeks, his jaw, down the side of his neck.

He raised his head to look at her, her name trembling on his lips.

But the face gazing back at him wasn't Emily's.

He woke with a small start, gazing up into darkness, his heart pounding wildly in his chest. At eye level, the pale blue light of an alarm clock displayed the time. 5:30 a.m.

Tucked into the curve of his body, Hannah's body was soft and warm. He could feel her slow, even breathing and knew she was still asleep.

The memory of their night of passion blurred with the dream that had wakened him, until he wasn't sure what was real and what was imagination. Was this really her body, fitted to his so perfectly it seemed they'd been chiseled from the same stone? Had their bodies found, instinctively, that perfect rhythm that lovers knew, the ebb and flow of control and submission that usually came from years of intimacy?

Had it been Hannah's face gazing back at him in his dream?

Carefully, he edged away from her. She stirred briefly but settled back into a deep, quiet sleep.

He rolled from the bed, grabbing his discarded boxers from the floor, and padded down the hall to the bathroom. He looked into the mirror over the sink, gazing curiously at the man who stared back at him in the glass.

He looked rested, he realized with surprise, despite the early hour and the exertions of the previous night. Stress lines that had creased his forehead had almost disappeared, only faint shadows marking the skin as a reminder of what had once been. His eyes looked clear, his gaze steady, devoid of pain for the first time in three long years.

About a year after Emily's murder, when his self-imposed isolation had begun to make him crazy, he'd gone to Jackson for a weekend, just to be around people who didn't know who he was or what he'd lost. It hadn't been hard to find a woman as uninterested in happily-ever-after as he had been. Trips to Jackson had become a regular thing for him, once or twice a month. Just to take the edge off.

The other nights, the other women—all had left their mark. But always for the worse. Never the better.

He turned off the light and went out into the hallway, pausing outside the bathroom. What should he do now? Go back to the bedroom, where Hannah lay warm and naked between his sheets? Or to the kitchen, to get an early start on figuring out how to talk Hannah out of her crazy, dangerous plan?

She made the decision for him, emerging from the guest room wearing nothing but his shirt.

She gave him a tentative smile. "Good morning."

Her hair was a dark tangle, framing her sleep-softened face. Her lips were pink and swollen from their kisses, and the skin of her throat was bright red from the rasp of his beard against her skin.

His body quickened in response, and he had nowhere to hide.

A slow, naughty smile spread over her sleepy face. She walked slowly down the hallway, her gaze locked with his. She stopped in front of him, lifting one hand to his chest.

"It's cold out here in the hallway." She slid her hand slowly down his belly, until her fingers tangled briefly in the waistband of his boxers, then dipped lower. "Why don't we go back to bed?"

He couldn't have said no if he wanted to.

THEY TOOK TURNS SHOWERING a couple of hours later, oddly hesitant to share that particular bit of intimacy. Maybe it was tacit acknowledgement, on both their parts, of how transient their intimacy really was.

Hannah went first, and by the time Riley emerged from the bathroom, dressed in clean jeans and a fresh, blue chambray shirt, she'd already brewed a pot of hot, strong coffee and was cracking eggs in a skillet on the stove.

"Two eggs or three?" she asked over her shoulder, trying not to picture the long, lean body hidden beneath the clothing. If she didn't get her mind out of the bedroom, how was she going to pull off her part of Sheriff Tanner's plan?

She couldn't afford to be off her game today.

"Three." Riley reached into the breadbox to pull out a loaf of wheat bread. "I'm making toast—want a piece?"

"Please." She cracked two more eggs into the pan and let them cook sunny side up. "Sheriff Tanner didn't call last night, did he? I didn't hear the phone ring."

"I checked while I was dressing. No messages." He sounded relieved.

"I'm sure he'll call soon." She said it gently, not wanting to sound defensive. She hadn't really expected a night of lovemaking to change Riley's mind about the plan to lure the killer into a trap. If anything, it probably made him even more determined to keep her out of danger.

It had certainly made her think twice about risking her life. The closeness to Riley she'd felt, far beyond the passion and pleasure, had shown her that she could still open herself to the possibility of love.

At least, she could with Riley, she amended silently. There was no guarantee she'd find this feeling again with another man. What if Riley were the one for her, the man she'd thought she'd found in Craig before reality proved otherwise?

It would be just her luck, she thought bleakly, to fall for a man who'd forever be in love with his dead wife.

Her appetite drained away, although she forced herself to work her way through the eggs and toast on her plate. Across from her, Riley ate with gusto, his gaze playing lightly over her face. Whenever their eyes met, he smiled, tempting her to believe he might not be as out of reach as she thought.

Fortunately, the phone rang before breakfast was over, dragging her back to sober reality. Riley answered, his expression immediately going grim. He held out the receiver. "Jim Tanner for you."

Hannah took the phone. "This is Hannah."

Jim Tanner got right down to business. "I've arranged for McCoy Edwards from Channel Twelve to interview you for the five o'clock news. You're to meet him at the station around 11:00 a.m. to pretape the segment. Can you be there?"

"Of course." She glanced at Riley. He watched her with stormy-blue eyes.

"In fact, have Patterson bring you to my office by ten-thirty. That way I can deliver you to the station myself. Riley can come along if he likes, but not in any official capacity. We don't want word getting around that you're under the protection of a Canyon Creek policeman."

"Will do," she agreed, and rang off soon after.

Riley hung up the phone for her and returned to the table, dropping into the chair across from her. "So, you're really going through with it?"

"Yes," she answered simply.

He sighed deeply, signaling his disagreement, and proceeded to finish breakfast in silence.

RILEY'S STOMACH WAS A SERIES of knots by the time they arrived at the television studio in Jackson. Sheriff Tanner had briefed Hannah on what to say and what not to say, and now the three of them piled out of the sheriff's Ford Bronco and entered the studio, where the television reporter, McCoy Edwards, was waiting to greet them.

Edwards was in his early fifties, with sharp, green eyes and thick, slicked-back dark hair edged with silver. He greeted the sheriff as if they were old friends, a feeling the sheriff clearly didn't share, and then pulled Hannah aside with a gentle tug once the introductions were over.

Riley watched them go, keeping his eye on Edwards as he led Hannah to a pair of chairs in front of a textured gray wall of a news set and settled her in with care. Riley could hear the murmur of their low conversation but couldn't make out any words. He turned to Tanner. "Are you sure you can trust him?"

"We need to get the story out to make this work. Edwards is the guy who can make it happen."

Not exactly the answer he'd hoped for, Riley thought, his gaze finding Hannah again. She looked in his direction, a tentative half-smile on her face. He knew she couldn't see much past the lights shining on her, but he smiled his encouragement anyway, even though his gut felt twisted inside-out.

Once they settled down to the interview, Riley could hear their words more clearly. To his credit, Edwards asked smart questions, and his follow-ups suggested he'd done his homework beyond reading Mark Archibald's article in the Jackson paper.

Finally, he got to the question Riley knew Hannah had been waiting for. "Do you think you'll ever remember everything about the event?"

"I don't know. But I'm going to see a doctor at Jackson Memorial tomorrow morning. She's a certified therapeutic hypnotist. I'm hoping we can work through some of the memory blocks so I can help the police even more."

Riley's heart clenched. With that one answer, she'd set the trap. Nothing left to do now but see it through to the end.

He just hoped Hannah was still standing when the smoke finally cleared.

"YOU STILL THINK I'M MAKING a mistake." Hannah stirred in Riley's arms, turning to face him. She couldn't see more than the shadowy outline of his face in the darkened bedroom, but she felt the tension build in his body at her words.

"I don't think it was a safe choice," he answered.

Such a careful response, she thought with as much affection as frustration. "I know it's not the safe choice. That doesn't mean it's not the right one."

His big hand found her face in the dark, his fingers tangling in her hair as he gave her a soft, slightly clumsy caress. "Depends on who you ask."

She twined her fingers with his and leaned in to kiss him. His mouth was hot and soft beneath hers, and the low simmer of heat in her belly flickered into flame. "I have to do this," she breathed against his lips.

"If you're doing it for me—"

"I told you already, it's as much for me as for you." She lay back against the pillow, closing her eyes.

"What if nothing happens?" he asked quietly. "What if he doesn't take the bait?"

Pain nipped at her heart. "Then I go home as planned."

"And I keep looking." He rolled on to his back until they lay side by side, no longer touching.

In the morning, Hannah thought, *I'll pack my bags so I'll be ready to catch the afternoon flight out of Jackson Hole. I'll be home tomorrow night, back in my little house by the lake with my crazy, enormous family surrounding me.*

But where would Riley be?

"If the plan works, and we catch him—what then?" she asked aloud. "What will you do?"

He didn't answer right away, though she could almost hear him thinking. After a moment, the bed shook as he gave a small shrug. "I don't know. I've never thought that far ahead."

She slipped her hand into his. "I hope you have to start thinking about it."

His fingers curled around hers, and she smiled sadly in the dark.

FROM HIS POSITION NEAR the front entrance, he spotted Sheriff Jim Tanner entering the hospital first. The clock on the wall over the information desk read 10:49 a.m.

Right on time. He'd checked the shrink's schedule earlier that morning, before she arrived, and found Hannah Cooper's name pencilled in at eleven.

Dressed in jeans and a denim jacket, the Teton County Sheriff was indistinguishable from the other visitors milling about the hospital lobby. Most people there probably didn't realize he was the sheriff.

But I'm not most people, he thought with a grim smile. Ever since the newscast the night before, he'd been expecting something just like this to happen.

As if he was stupid enough to fall for so obvious a set-up.

He could imagine the sheriff's reasoning. *He's escalating. Time is running out to get to her. He'll be desperate enough to take a big risk.* All that psychobabble cops pulled out of their backsides when they didn't know what would happen next.

He'd applied to the FBI a while back. He knew all about that sort of thinking, the tricks the G-Man types pulled to make people think they were smarter than they really were.

But they hadn't been smart enough to hire him, had they?

Movement to his right caught his eye. His heartbeat kicked up a notch. There she was, as expected, walking slowly toward the entrance. A few feet in front of the glass doors, she hesitated, just a moment. A surge of pure pleasure rushed through him at the sight of her unease.

I'm in your head, aren't I, sweet baby?

As he watched, her chin came up, her shoulders squared and she entered the hospital lobby. Her renewed resolve did nothing to dampen his enjoyment, however. He liked a challenge.

She walked past where the sheriff sat, not even giving him a glance. Heading straight to the elevators, she punched the up button.

As she disappeared inside, the new guy, Sanchez, strolled up next to him. He smiled pleasantly. "Boss sent me down here to learn the ropes, would you believe? Like I've never walked security before. I worked county lock-up, for God's sake."

So had he, though not in Teton County. He'd put in his time as a prison guard in Natrona, a few years back.

Sanchez nodded his head to the right, his meaty brow furrowed. "Hey, is that the sheriff?"

He just smiled.

"I ADMIT, THIS IS ONE OF MY stranger moments as a therapist." Dr. Janis Templeton smiled at Hannah across her wide, oak desk. "I've never been part of a police sting before. I can't decide if it's exciting or nerve racking."

Hannah smiled back, though her stomach had been in knots all morning. "If it makes you feel better, neither can I."

"How long before you know if it worked?"

"I'm supposed to stay the hour. Then I walk through the hospital alone and meet the sheriff downstairs in the lobby." Hannah glanced at her watch. She'd been in Dr. Templeton's office for only ten minutes. It had felt much longer.

Dr. Templeton sat back in her chair, crossing her legs. She was only a little older than Hannah, maybe in her early thirties. She was pretty in a natural sort of way, with minimal makeup and a short, unfussy hairstyle that suited her. Her suit was simple but well cut, showing off her slim swimmer's build. Hannah wondered if she had much chance to swim in a place like Jackson, Wyoming.

"I suppose while we're here, it wouldn't hurt to talk to you a bit about your memory loss. Has anything come back at all?" Dr. Templeton asked.

"A few things. I don't know what I'm at liberty to tell you, though."

Dr. Templeton nodded. "Of course. I was just wondering if you'd seriously considered hypnosis to recover some of the missing pieces."

"Not really." Hannah gave her an apologetic look. "One of my brothers is a prosecutor, and he's not a big fan of hypnotherapy as a means of recovering repressed memories."

"He's thinking as a litigator—what can be used in court. I'm talking about a relaxation technique to let your mind do its job without any interference." Dr. Templeton picked up a pencil on her desk and ran it between her slim fingers. "You clearly want to remember more or you wouldn't be here risking your safety. Maybe you should consider contacting a hypnotherapist when you get back home."

"I'll think about it," Hannah said, although she wasn't comfortable with the idea.

"Meanwhile, we might as well enjoy the next twenty minutes," Dr. Templeton said with a smile. "Why don't you tell me more about yourself?"

"DO WE HAVE A MASTER LIST of the personnel on duty this morning?" Riley asked Jim Tanner as they settled into chairs in the hospital lobby. Joe Garrison sat nearby, within earshot.

"The hospital administrator sent it by fax this morning." Tanner opened his briefcase and pulled out a printed spreadsheet. "Since the five o'clock news aired, seven employees called in sick. Two nurse's aides, one orderly, a cafeteria worker, a doctor and two nurses."

"Nobody in security?" Joe asked.

"Everybody reported as scheduled." Tanner passed a sheet

of paper to Riley. "I typed their names up for you, since I know you think security is the weak link."

Riley scanned the list of names. "This is a new one," he said, pointing out one of the names near the bottom.

"Yeah, Mike Sanchez. He's a retired county-jail guard. He wasn't ready to be put out to pasture, so I vouched for him here at the hospital." Tanner raised his eyes and gave the lobby a quick scan. "He's a little on the husky side these days. Doesn't fit your girl's description."

My girl, Riley thought with a pang. They'd certainly spent the last two nights wrapped up in each other like lovers.

He glanced at his watch. "It's nearly noon. She'll be coming down any minute." Every muscle in his body felt like a rubber band stretched taut, ready to snap. He forced himself to breathe slowly and evenly, trying to regain control. The Ruger tucked into the holster hidden beneath his leather jacket felt heavy against his hip.

He knew there were two undercover Teton County deputies on the third floor, where the psychiatrist's office was located. One of them had been assigned to follow Hannah into the elevator for the ride down to the lobby. He, Joe and Jim Tanner were in charge of getting her safely out of the lobby.

He should be hoping for the killer to make a move. With so many officers on the lookout, the guy would be a sitting duck.

But Riley couldn't wish Hannah danger. He'd rather spend the rest of his life chasing the bastard.

With a soft ding, the nearest elevator opened and Hannah emerged. A moment later, the sandy-haired undercover deputy came out behind her. The deputy locked gazes with the sheriff and gave a slight shake of his head.

The plan had failed.

Hannah walked up to where they sat, slumping into the empty seat by Riley. "No luck, it seems."

Riley slid his arm around the back of her chair. "Depends on who you're asking," he murmured.

The look she gave him was a blend of disappointment and affection. "So, I guess the next stop is the airport."

His heart sank. They'd packed her bags and put them in the truck before leaving the house that morning. Her flight left the Jackson Hole airport around three, so there'd be no time to return to the house.

This was it. His last hours with her.

Sheriff Tanner stood up, cuing them to do the same. Riley settled his hand at the small of Hannah's back and walked out with her as she followed Tanner and Joe outside to the parking lot. He stayed alert crossing the lot to their vehicles, in case their unidentified suspect decided to make one last play to take Hannah down.

But the walk was uneventful.

At the truck, Tanner turned to Hannah, holding out his hand. "It's been a pleasure meeting you, Ms. Cooper. You have a safe trip home, and I'll be in touch if anything comes up on the case." He nodded to Riley and Joe and headed for his Bronco parked a few slots over.

Hannah turned to Joe. "Thank you for all your help, Joe. And please tell Jane again how much I appreciated her help when I arrived. She promised to e-mail me when the baby gets here. You make sure she does, okay?"

"I'll do that. Have a safe flight." Joe gave her a quick hug and met Riley's gaze over her shoulder, a thousand questions in his eyes.

Questions Riley couldn't have answered if he wanted to.

After Joe left, Hannah turned to look at Riley, her expression as bleak as a Wyoming winter. "We'd better hit the road. Jane said it's a bit of a drive to the airport."

He helped her into the truck cab and went around to the driver's side. "It's a little ways," he agreed, "but we'll have a good view of the mountains."

She buckled herself in. "I'm sorry the plan didn't work."

"I'm not," he said, and meant it.

She turned her head and gazed at him with moist eyes. "I just wanted this to be over for you. It doesn't feel right to be going home and leaving you here still searching for answers."

Then stay, he thought. But he couldn't say the words aloud. What he could offer her, at best, was half a man, and she deserved so much more than that.

They stopped for burgers on the trip to the airport, eating in silence, each knowing that everything that could be said between them already had. They didn't speak again until he parked in the short-term parking at the airport and carried her luggage for her to the check-in area.

She turned to look at him, her green eyes dark with sadness. "I won't make you go through security just to see me off. It'll just make me all weepy and stuffed up for the flight, and who needs that at thirty-thousand feet, right?" She managed a watery grin.

He cradled her face between his hands. "You have my phone number. Call when you get home so I know you got there safely."

She nodded, still smiling through her tears.

"Are you sure you don't want me to contact the local authorities to give you some protection?"

"My brother's a deputy. Two of my other brothers are auxiliary deputies. I have a rifle of my own. I'll be fine. Besides, he's not likely to follow me all the way back to Alabama, is he?"

Tamping down his fears and regrets, he brushed his lips to hers, not daring anything more, and then crushed her against him, holding her tightly. "Thank you for everything," he murmured into her ear.

He let her go and stepped back, his heartbeat playing a slow dirge against his ribcage. He wanted to say more, to explain to her how much he regretted seeing her go, but he'd long ago learned the difference between what he wanted and what had to be. So he gave her a quick smile that he hoped conveyed how much he was going to miss her and turned toward the exit.

Reaching the door, he looked back one more time to find her standing where he'd left her, her heart in her eyes.

Mustering all the strength he had, he turned and walked out the door.

Chapter Fifteen

Her timing was lousy all the way around.

If she'd gone to Wyoming in the spring, she could have returned to a wildly busy office to take her mind off everything she went through on her vacation. The past week would have been a whirlwind of fishing-camp bookings, clients looking to schedule guided fishing trips, and several of her brothers running in and out of the office between fishing trips and maintenance calls.

But by late October, the season was coming to an end, and the phone calls slowed to a trickle, leaving her too much time to think about Riley and the way things between them had ended.

Maybe it would have been easier if their brief fling had blown up in a huge, dramatic fight. At least there would have been passion, tears and the chance to get good and mad. But watching him walk away, knowing with every cell in her body that he felt the same connection between them that she did, had been a sort of quiet, relentless torture she hadn't yet escaped.

She pushed back her desk chair and crossed to the filing cabinet on the pretense that there was something in the office she hadn't filed in the week since she returned home. But the cabinet was immaculately organized, thanks to her desperate attempt to keep her mind off Riley for the past seven days.

Admitting defeat, she slammed the drawer shut and turned around to look at the empty office.

The phone rang, an unexpected reprieve. She hurried to answer it. "Cooper Cove Properties."

"Hey, Skipper, it's me." It was her brother Aaron, using her much-hated childhood nickname because he liked to hear her growl. But this time, her heart wasn't in it.

"Hey, what's up besides the crime rate?"

"You're funny," he retorted. "It's down, for your information."

"In spite of you?" she teased, knowing how much he prided himself on his job as a Chickasaw County Sheriff's Deputy.

"Because of me, naturally." He took the teasing with good humor. He was the youngest, except for her, which had often made them natural allies over the years. "But that's not why I called. Have you talked to Mom yet?"

From the excited tone in his voice, she guessed it wasn't bad news. "No—what's going on?"

"Sam's moving back home."

"Officially?" She grinned. "When?"

"He got the job he wanted in the Jefferson County District Attorney's office."

Some of her excitement faded. "But Birmingham's an hour away. We won't ever get to see Maddy."

"The job is an hour away, but he's going to commute. He's already got his eye on a house on Mission Road in town. Nice place—I swung by to take a look for him. Nice big yard, easy drive to the lake. It's perfect."

"Tell him to take it!" The more brothers to distract her from her miserable life, the better.

"I plan to." Aaron's voice softened. "So, how are you really doing?"

The concern in his voice made tears prick her eyes. She blinked them back. "I'm good. The concussion was nearly two weeks ago."

"I'm not talking about the concussion. It had to be unnerving to be on a serial killer's hit list."

"It was, but I'm home now, safe and sound, and if there's any justice, the cops in Wyoming will have him behind bars any day now."

"They haven't got him yet."

She frowned at the phone. "And you'd know that how?"

"I might have given the Teton County sheriff a call this morning," he admitted.

She couldn't decide if she was relieved or disappointed that he hadn't called Riley instead. "But they're still on it, right?"

"Absolutely. And the sheriff thinks you should be perfectly safe now that you're home."

"Good to hear." The office door opened and Mariah entered, waggling her fingers at Hannah. "Listen, Mariah just got here, and you need to get back to work. Great news about Sam. Now if we could just get Luke home, I'd have all my ducks in a row."

She winced a little, mentally, at her choice of words. Riley had said something very like that to her, at a time that now felt like a lifetime ago. She ruthlessly shoved the memory out of her mind and rang off. "That was Aaron," she told Mariah.

"He told you about your brother coming home, no?" Mariah laid her backpack on her desk and smiled at Hannah. "Jake told me the news. I can't wait to meet him."

"That's right, you haven't met him or Luke yet." Mariah and Hannah's brother Jake had met less than a year earlier, and eloped to Gatlinburg a couple of months after that. At the time, Hannah had secretly questioned whether a marriage based on two months' acquaintance was a good idea, but after almost eight months, they seemed to be working out well.

And after Wyoming, she didn't have much room to talk.

Mariah smiled at Hannah again, but as always, the smile didn't quite overcome the sadness always present in her coffee-colored eyes. She'd been a widow with a small child when she met Hannah's brother Jake, and it seemed even her obvious love for her new husband hadn't quite erased that sense of loss. "It's odd to have such a large family. Back in Texas, there were only my parents and me."

"Having seven kids is pretty odd these days, no matter where you're from." Hannah grinned.

Mariah settled behind her desk and pushed papers around the blotter, no doubt looking for something constructive to do. Hannah was about to tell her to use her time doing homework or reading ahead for her next class when Mariah looked up shyly, a faint blush staining her olive skin.

"I've been thinking about something you told me. About the case in Wyoming." Her lightly accented English had a musical quality that Hannah always found soothing. "You said you saw a psychiatrist in Wyoming—a hypnotherapist?"

"Right—when we tried to set the trap for the guy, the cover story was that I was seeing a hypnotherapist to recover missing memories." Hannah smiled. "It reminded me of you and your hypnosis tricks."

Mariah's smile was tinged with thoughtfulness. "It is not so much a trick, actually. It is a way to let your mind relax and open. Perhaps you really should try it."

The thought still gave her the willies. She took such pride in her self-control that losing it, even a little, was frightening.

But courage was about doing the right thing, even in the face of fear, wasn't it?

She didn't want to think of herself as a coward.

"What do you need to do it?" she asked aloud. "Can we do it right here and now?"

Mariah's eyebrows notched upwards, but she gave a quick nod. "I think I can find something—" She dug through her desk drawer until she emerged with a yellow pencil. "This will work. Come, let's go to the conference room."

Hannah followed Mariah to the small sitting room that served as the booking office's conference room. Mariah motioned for her to sit in the cozy armchair, while she took a seat on the sofa across from her.

"The main thing I want you to do is breathe. In and out, slow and steady." As she spoke, Mariah tapped the eraser end of the pencil rhythmically on the coffee table.

Dr. Pendleton had done something very similar when Hannah was talking to her in her office, she remembered. Had it been an attempt to ease Hannah's obvious tension?

"Close your eyes, clear your mind and concentrate on breathing in tempo with my taps," Mariah said.

Hannah did as Mariah asked, focusing on the slow, steady intake and exhale of air in rhythm with the tapping pencil. After a few moments, her limbs began to feel heavy.

"You are relaxed and open. You are aware of everything around you. There is nothing you have seen or heard that you cannot access. Do you believe me when I say that?"

She did, Hannah realized. "Yes."

"Good. Because all we're doing here is answering questions. Answer them as well as you can. No pressure at all. Now, I want you to remember the day you were attacked. Was it a sunny day?"

"Yes, but it was late afternoon. The sun was dropping behind the mountains and there were shadows all around me." She saw the road spreading out in front of her, the endless wilderness on either side of the highway.

"When did you notice the car?"

"I checked my rearview mirror and there he was."

"What did the car look like?"

"It was big. A sedan. I think it might have been dark blue. I really only noticed the blue light on the roof."

"Did you see the man inside the car?"

"No. The windshield was darkened." Had she told the police in Wyoming about the tinted windows? She felt herself begin to tense up.

"Breathe, Hannah. When we are done, you can ask yourself the questions that make you anxious, but for now, the anxiety is gone. Breathe it away."

Hannah did as Mariah told her, and soon the tension passed.

"He came to your car. What were you doing as he was walking toward you?"

"I was getting my license and registration information."

"Did you glance in any of the mirrors to see what he looked like?" Mariah asked.

"No. It happened so fast—he was there within seconds."

"What did you do when you found the license and registration papers?"

"I turned to the window." Anticipating Mariah's next question, she added, "He was already right by the car. All I could see was his shirt, his midsection and his hand. I saw his belt buckle—a rattlesnake." Funny how clear it was in her head now. "His belt was brown leather. No markings."

"Was the pepper spray in his hand?"

"Yes. He was wearing latex gloves. I got a brief glimpse

before—" She stopped as she replayed the moment in her head and saw something she hadn't remembered before. "He used both hands to spray the pepper spray, almost like a two-handed shooting stance. I'd forgotten that. And on his left pinky finger he wore a ring."

"You could see it through the gloves?"

"Yes. It was gold with a black stone and a small gold inset on the stone." She opened her eyes and looked at Mariah, excitement building. "I can't believe I didn't remember that. I mean, when I slammed my elbow down on his fingers to get away, I felt the ring crack against my funny bone."

Mariah put the pencil down on the table and regarded her solemnly. "Do you remember what the gold inset was?"

Hannah broke into a broad smile. "It was a horseshoe."

NEARLY 30,000 FEET BELOW, Missouri looked like a tiny relief map, criss-crossed by rivers and streams snaking west from the Mississippi River. He was still a few hours away from landing in Nashville, but from there, the drive to Gossamer Ridge, Alabama, would take less than three hours. He planned to stay overnight in Nashville and get an early start on the road.

He had to get to Gossamer Ridge for a morning rendezvous.

She'd been quite helpful, really, telling the newspaper reporter all about her life in Alabama. The family marina, running the booking office, even her quirky little side job as a fishing guide. He supposed she did that alone, too.

Reckless woman.

He'd used this past week not only to prepare for his cross-country trip but also to let the police—and Hannah Cooper—develop a false sense of security. They didn't expect him to go to such lengths to tie up loose ends. Wouldn't fit the profile, he thought with a smile.

As the flight attendant passed, she smiled back at him. For a moment, he imagined what it would be like to have her on his table in the basement of his mother's house. To watch her twist and writhe as her fate became clearer, to realize that her own actions had led her to that place and that outcome.

But the flight attendant hadn't earned that punishment, had she? At least, not yet. She hadn't ignored his warnings and sealed her fate.

Hannah Cooper had, however. And he wasn't one to leave things unfinished.

RILEY GAZED AT THE PAPERS spread across his desk and saw none of them. He'd spent most of the past week in this same position, hunched forward over his desk, moving papers around like pieces of a jigsaw puzzle in the pretense that his mind was still on the work and not hundreds of miles away in the hills of northeast Alabama.

New information had come in on the case, most of it eliminating suspects rather than pinpointing anyone in particular. Among the hospital security personnel, only five possibles remained. None of them looked very promising, but they still remained more likely than the other hospital staffers they'd also been looking at.

He picked up the background sheets on the possibles, trying to concentrate on finding something he'd missed the first ten times he'd looked at these sheets over the past week, but all he could see was Hannah's shattered expression when he'd turned around in the airport terminal to look at her for the last time.

He should have asked her to stay. Or hell, offered to go with her. What was keeping him here anymore, except an unhealthy craving for revenge? His parents were in Arizona. Jack was God knew where.

And Emily was dead.

But he wasn't. He may have felt as if he were a walking corpse for the past three years, but he wasn't dead yet. He still had years ahead of him, and living them as if life held no joy at all was the worst possible tribute to Emily's memory.

For the first time, he felt her censure, the full truth of the words Joe had told him just a few short days ago.

Emily would hate what you're becoming.

The buzzer on his desk phone sounded. "Riley—get in here." It was Joe, and he sounded excited.

He headed into Joe's office and found him on the phone. Joe held up a finger and finished the conversation. "Yes, I think it'll be very helpful. For sure it gives us another piece of the puzzle to help us cull suspects. I'll definitely let you know if anything comes of it. Bye, now." Joe hung up and looked at Riley, clearly excited but also exhibiting tell-tale signs of guilt.

"Who was that?" Riley asked, although in his sinking heart he knew the answer.

"Hannah Cooper," Joe answered, sending a sliver of pain slicing straight through Riley's heart. "She remembered something else."

Riley listened as Joe told him about how Hannah had let her sister-in-law hypnotize her and remembered a ring the killer had been wearing, but all he could think about was the fact that Hannah had called Joe and not him.

No surprise, really. After all, he'd broken her heart. He'd known it even as he was doing it. Why would she ever want to speak to him again?

Yet she'd obviously kept thinking about the case, enough to let her sister-in-law hypnotize her into remembering more.

"I need time off," he said bluntly.

Joe looked at him as if he'd lost his mind. "I just told you we got a break in the case, and you want time off?"

Riley stood, propelled by a restless urgency that grew stronger each second he remained in this office. He'd been headed toward this moment for a week, hadn't he? Every moment spent thinking about her, rewinding every touch, every conversation, every regret for seven endless, excruciating days.

"She could have gone home and not given this case another thought," he said aloud. "After all she went through, I wouldn't have blamed her for it. But she didn't."

A slow smile of understanding spread across Joe's face. "You're going to Alabama, aren't you?"

Riley grinned back at him, suddenly feeling the urge to laugh aloud. "Yes, I believe I am."

"Well, I'm going to pass this information along to Sheriff Tanner and see if any of the Memorial Hospital staff wears an onyx pinky ring with a gold horseshoe set into it. You go book a flight and get packed."

"Call me on my cell if you get any breaks in the case," Riley said over his shoulder, already halfway out the door.

He found a flight leaving around 4:30 p.m. from Casper arriving in Birmingham before midnight and booked a room for a night at a motel not far from the Interstate. Packing in a rush, he was on the road to Casper by noon.

In twenty-four hours, he'd be with Hannah again. And if he was lucky, and she was forgiving, he wouldn't ever be without her again.

HANNAH WAS LOCKING UP at the booking office late that afternoon when the phone rang. She glanced at the caller identification display, ready to blow off anyone she wasn't in the mood to talk to. But the number had a Tennessee area code. Might be a client. She answered. "Cooper Cove Properties."

"Hi, there." The voice was male and friendly, with a neutral accent Hannah couldn't place, though it sounded vaguely familiar. "My name is Ken Lassiter, and I was hoping you might have an opening in your schedule tomorrow morning for a guided crappie-fishing tour."

She pretended to grab her book, although the truth was, hardly anyone was fishing for crappie on Gossamer Lake this time of year. No matter—she knew good spots to fish any time of the year. "I have an availability first thing in the morning. Can you be here by 6:30 a.m.?"

"I certainly can," Lassiter answered cheerfully. "Are you the one who'll be taking me?"

"That's right." She braced for a change of heart. Some men didn't like being guided by women.

"Do I need to bring my own tackle?"

She relaxed. Apparently, Mr. Lassiter wasn't one of those men. "Not unless you want to. We provide all the tackle and gear as part of the service." She named a price. "That will get you a full day on the lake. Half a day, half price. You pay up front at the bait shop by the docks. I'll be here when you arrive."

"Let's go with half a day. I'm betting we can get the job done by then," Lassiter said. "I didn't get your name—"

"Cooper. Hannah Cooper."

"I look forward to fishing with you, Ms. Cooper. I'll see you at six-thirty." Lassiter rang off, and Hannah wrote the appointment down in the book.

As she finished locking up the office, she found herself looking forward to getting back on the lake. If anything could take her mind off Riley Patterson and Wyoming, it was a day of crappie fishing on Gossamer Lake.

HE HUNG UP THE PAY PHONE outside a store within sight of the Metro Riverfront Park. The late afternoon was pleasantly mild for October; he was glad he'd thought to pack clothes for a warmer climate. Around him, locals and tourists mingled along the city sidewalks, heading for their cars parked along the busy streets or for the bus stop near the river.

Nobody gave him a second look, which was why he'd chosen this place, miles from his motel room, to make his call to the Cooper Cove Marina.

Hearing her voice had been an electric shock to his system. The week he'd given her to relax her guard had been harder on him than he'd realized. While he prided himself on his self-control, he'd never really been one to deny himself necessary pleasures.

And seeing Hannah Cooper again would be a pleasure, indeed.

Chapter Sixteen

Saturday morning turned out to be sunny and mild, warm for mid-October. Hannah would have preferred to be out on the lake by sunrise, but today she was on the clock for a paying client, so she played by his rules.

She brewed a pot of coffee at home and poured it into a sturdy thermos in case the client needed a little caffeine to get him going in the morning. She'd packed her boat with all the necessary rods and tackle the night before, and her father had culled out four dozen minnows, ready to stow in the boat's bait well in case the client wanted to fish with live bait.

Her parents were already at work at the bait shop when she arrived. "Are you sure you want to take this one by yourself?" her father asked her, worry in his eyes. "It's so soon after—"

"It's a fishing trip. I've been doing these by myself for years," she assured him, giving him a quick kiss on the cheek. He smelled like Old Spice and mint toothpaste, the scents familiar and comforting, reminding her that she was safely home, surrounded by a loving, fiercely protective family.

"I went ahead and put the minnows in the bait well for you," he said. "And J.D. gassed it up for you last night, so you should be ready to go."

Car headlights sliced through the early-morning gloom outside the bait shop.

"Must be your client," her mother said.

Anxiety slithered through her belly at the sound of footsteps crunching the gravel outside. She wrestled it into submission and pasted a welcoming smile on her face as the sandy-haired man in his early thirties entered the bait shop and flashed them a friendly smile.

"Ms. Cooper?" The man held out his hand. "Ken Lassiter."

She shook his hand firmly. "Good morning, Mr. Lassiter."

"Ken, please. I can call you Hannah?"

"Of course." She walked around the counter to the cash register. "We can take all major credit cards, or cash. We don't take checks from out of state."

"Cash is fine." Reaching into his pocket, he pulled out a folded stack of bills and placed them on the counter. Hannah rang up the service and thanked him.

"How long have you been guiding?" he asked once they had boarded her small, sleek Triton TC 17 and settled in for the ride across the lake to one of her favorite fall crappie spots.

"Since I got my boating license about twelve years ago," she answered, raising her voice above the roar of the Mercury outboard. "I grew up on the lake, so I've been fishing since I could hold a cane pole."

Ken flashed her a quick smile, then looked back out over the lake. "Quiet this morning."

"A lot of the boats are already out this time of day."

"Are we going to be rubbing elbows with a lot of other fishermen, then?" he asked, looking a little disappointed.

"Not where I'm taking you," she assured him.

The wind was brisk and cool as they skimmed the green

waters of Gossamer Lake, but she knew it would warm up once they dropped anchor and started trolling for the quirky little speckled-white fish they were after this morning. Meanwhile, the loamy smell of the lake and the rosy glow of the morning sky gave her a giddy feeling of well-being, the first glimpse of her normal self since she returned home from Wyoming.

She should have come out fishing sooner. It had always been her favorite way of centering her world.

Maybe she'd get Riley Patterson out of her heart yet.

RILEY'S CELL PHONE RANG around 7:00 a.m., while he was in the motel bathroom about to shave. He fished the phone out of the pocket of his jeans. It was Joe's cell number. "Yeah?"

"Where are you?" The tension in Joe's voice set Riley's nerves immediately on edge.

"Budget Suites Motel in Birmingham." He headed out of the bathroom, shaving forgotten. "What's going on?"

"How long will it take you to get to Gossamer Ridge?"

"Hour and a half, I think—what's going on?"

The brief pause on the other end of the line made Riley's empty stomach cramp. It was almost a relief when Joe spoke. "I think we've found the killer."

Riley dropped heavily on to the bed. "Who?"

"Guy named Kyle Layton. Six-one, early thirties, sandy-blond hair, gray eyes. A security guard at Memorial Hospital."

"Someone recognized the ring," Riley guessed.

"He wears it on his left pinky finger, like Hannah said."

"Can we connect him to our other cases?"

"We can connect him to at least one, I'm pretty sure," Joe answered grimly. "He was working as a prison guard in the Casper area when Emily was killed. He was one of the ones in charge of taking prisoners to the hospital where she worked when they couldn't handle their injuries or illnesses at the prison infirmary."

"Son of a bitch." Riley curled his hand into a fist as bleak rage poured into his gut like acid. "Tell me you have him in custody, Joe."

"He boarded a plane out of Casper yesterday morning around 9:00 a.m.," Joe answered. "Headed for Nashville, Tennessee."

"Tennessee?" It took a moment for Riley to get it. "Oh, hell."

"It's less than a three-hour drive to Gossamer Ridge. We've been able to ascertain that he spent the night at the motel in Nashville, but none of the staff has seen him this morning, and he's not in his room."

Riley lurched off the bed, swiping his keys and his holstered Ruger off the dresser. He shrugged on his jacket, snapped the holster to the waistband of his jeans and grabbed his hat on his way out the door. He took the steps down to the rental car two at a time. "I need you to get the Chickasaw County Sheriff's Department on the phone. Ask for—" He grimaced. What the hell was the brother's name? "Ask for a Cooper. I can't remember the name."

"I'm on it."

"If you get him, tell him to find his sister and keep her in one place until I can get there. And give him my cell number." Riley rang off and jerked the rental car into gear, startling a maintenance staffer who was out picking up garbage in the cool of the early morning.

Punching the number of Hannah's cell phone into his cell phone as he sped up the on-ramp to I-59, he muttered a fervent prayer that she'd answer. But her voicemail connected after two rings. "Hannah, it's Riley. If you get this, find your parents or one of your brothers and stick with them until I get there. I'm in Birmingham but I'm heading your way. Do not go anywhere alone, do you hear me? We've found the killer. His name is Kyle Layton." He rattled off the description Joe had given him. "He's on his way to Alabama."

The voicemail beeped, cutting him off. He cursed and considered calling back but decided he'd been able to record enough to warn her to stay put. He tried directory assistance next and got the phone number for the Cooper Cove Marina booking office, but voicemail kicked in at that number as well. He left a similar message and rang off, a slow, sick terror rising like bile in his throat.

Where the hell was she? Was he already too late?

He was somewhere just past Gadsden, about five miles from the Gossamer Ridge exit and driving as fast as he dared when his cell phone rang. He grabbed it, not even checking the display. "Riley Patterson."

"This is Aaron Cooper. Hannah's brother." The voice on the other end of the line was low and tense. "Joe Garrison gave me your number."

"Tell me Hannah's with you right now," Riley demanded.

"She's not. She's out on the lake with a client."

The knots in Riley's stomach twisted into new knots. "A client?"

"I talked to my parents. She and a fishing client left around six-thirty this morning. Guy named Ken Lassiter."

"Six-one, sandy-blond hair, gray eyes?"

On the other end of the line, Aaron let loose a stream of profanities. "It's him, isn't it?"

"Yes. Do you have any idea where she'd take him?"

"One or two. I'm about ten minutes away from the lake. I'll call my brothers. They're probably already on the lake with clients. How far away are you?"

"I'm taking the Gossamer Ridge exit now," he said, jerking the rental car hard right and down the off-ramp.

"You're only a couple of miles from the turn-off to the marina. Take a left and watch for the sign on your left. You may beat me there, but wait for me!" Aaron rang off.

Though bleakly certain it was a futile gesture, Riley tried Hannah's cell number again. Voicemail again. He snapped the phone shut with a growl and took a left at the bottom of the ramp, shooting through a yellow light and hoping like hell there weren't any speed traps between him and the marina.

Hannah was on the lake with a killer, and he might already be too late.

HANNAH SLOWLY STEERED the Triton with the stick, watching her client twitch the jig around the edge of the sunken pier. This was one of her favorite fishing holes, but so far Ken Lassiter wasn't having much luck. He lacked the smooth, instinctive rhythm of an experienced crappie fisherman, but so far he'd refused her suggestion that he switch to live bait.

"Where are you from, Mr. Lassiter?" she asked, bringing the boat to a stop and unreeling the anchor until she felt it thump lightly on the muddy lake bottom.

"Idaho." He flashed her a rueful smile. "Not a lot of crappie fishing up there, I'm afraid."

"I was next door in Wyoming a couple of weeks ago," she commented, watching him cast the jig toward shore. "Good trout fishing there."

"Yes." He glanced at her. "Vacation or work?"

"Vacation," she answered, wishing she hadn't brought up Wyoming. It reminded her of Riley, and she was supposed to be putting Riley out of her head.

"Nice country, Wyoming. Where'd you go — Yellowstone? Did you see Old Faithful?"

"Didn't quite make it there."

"Do you go out by yourself like this all the time?" he asked over his shoulder.

"Usually. It's a small boat. Not a lot of room for extra passengers."

"You must be brave. It's a dangerous world out there."

The sound of his voice echoed in her head, drawing out a memory. A man's voice, neutral and low. Familiar. *"It's a dangerous world out there. You shouldn't be driving all by yourself. Anything could happen to you."*

Blood rushed loudly in her ears, making her feel light-headed. She gripped the seat of her chair and stared at Ken Lassiter's back, the horrible truth sliding relentlessly through the fog of first panic.

Ken Lassiter. Like the Lassiter Oil station where a mysterious man warned her not to travel alone, then punished her for not taking his advice.

She fought to remember what the man had looked like, desperate to convince herself that everything unfolding before her now was just some crazy coincidence. But her fishing client was the right height, the right build, and as far as she could remember, the right coloring. Today, just as he had that day at the gas station, he wore a baseball cap low over his forehead.

Just then, he lifted the spinning rod, giving her a close-up view of his left hand. A pale band of skin circled his pinky finger between the second and third knuckles, contrasting sharply with the rest of the tanned skin of his hand.

It was him. That's where the onyx ring went, the one he'd been wearing the day he'd attacked her.

In the back of her mind, a terrified voice was shrieking with panic, trying to drown out her attempts at logical thought. She beat it back with ruthless determination, taking advantage of the man's distraction to gather her wits.

She mentally raced through her options, not liking any of them. If this man was the killer, anything she did out of the ordinary, like ending their fishing trip abruptly, might spur him into action sooner. Trying to subdue him alone wasn't smart, either. He outweighed her by a lot, and there would be little room to maneuver on the boat to seek any sort of advantage.

And she didn't know how long she had before he decided to make his move. She wasn't sure why he hadn't made it already.

"Why don't we try another spot?" she suggested. "Maybe we'll have more luck there." She tried to keep the fear from her voice but wasn't sure she was succeeding.

"Let's stick here a little longer," he said calmly.

Hannah darted her gaze around the boat until she spotted her open tackle box. Beneath the upper trays, she had a nice big fillet knife stored, but getting to it would cause too much of a clamor and might draw his attention. However, if she could get to her jacket, which she'd shed when the temperature had risen with full sun-up, she could sneak out the sturdy pocketknife she always carried when she fished.

She stepped lightly to the middle of the boat and picked up the jacket, slipping it on.

Her movement caught Ken's attention. "Cold?"

"Just a little. The breeze has kicked up a bit." She snugged the jacket around her, sticking her hands in her pockets. She palmed the pocketknife, trying not to notice how small it felt.

If she could get him out of this secluded cove, she could track down Jake or Gabe at one of their favorite bass spots, she realized as the small comfort of the knife helped clear her mind a little. Both of her brothers were on the lake with fishing clients this morning. If she could reach one of them, she'd be safe. Then she could set the local cops on Ken Lassiter.

"Are you sure you don't want to head for another spot?" she asked again.

"Very." Lassiter turned around to look at her. "I have to say, Hannah Cooper, you're a hard woman to kill."

A CHICKASAW COUNTY SHERIFF'S cruiser sat in the parking lot of the Cooper Cove Bait Shop when Riley pulled in, his rental car kicking up gravel as he skidded to a stop. He rushed past the empty cruiser and entered the bait shop.

At the front, an older couple and a uniformed deputy turned to look at him.

"I'm Riley Patterson," he announced. "You're Aaron?"

The dark-haired deputy nodded. "These are my parents, Beth and Mike. We've tried calling my brothers on the lake, but they usually forward their calls to voicemail when they're fishing with clients. I was about to grab a boat and head out myself."

"Is that man really here?" the woman asked. Riley gave her a closer look, his heart clutching as he saw how much she looked like her daughter.

"Yes, ma'am. But we're going to stop him."

"I'm going with you," the older man said.

"No, Dad, you need to stay here with Mom." Aaron didn't say the rest of what he was clearly thinking. If Kyle Layton managed to kill Hannah, he might come back to the bait shop to tie up the rest of his loose ends.

"You're right," Mr. Cooper agreed, fear and rage battling it out in his expression.

"My boat's here." Aaron's terse, impatient voice drew Riley's attention back to the deputy. "You coming?"

Aaron led him on a weaving race through a maze of narrow

docks to a mid-sized powerboat near the end of one of the piers. He jumped in, and Riley followed, settling into the passenger seat. He pulled the Ruger from his holster and checked the clip. He had a second clip in his jacket pocket.

He hoped he wouldn't need either.

"Her phone's set to go automatically to voicemail," Aaron called over the roar of the outboard motor. "But I think I know where she'd have started fishing."

Assuming Kyle Layton let her get that far before making his move, Riley thought grimly.

"Hey!" Aaron suddenly started waving wildly at another boat. Riley followed the direction of his gaze and saw a bass boat skimming across the lake. The driver apparently spotted Aaron's signal and throttled down, easing the bass boat across the water until he came up beside Aaron's boat.

A tall man in his early thirties sat behind the steering wheel, a quizzical expression on his face. Another brother, Riley realized, seeing the resemblance to Hannah.

"What're you flagging me down for, doofus?" He nodded to a slightly sunburned man watching curiously from the passenger bench behind him. "I've got a client."

"Hannah's in trouble, Jake."

Jake's expression immediately shifted. "Where? What's happened?"

"That guy from Wyoming who attacked her—we think he's with her, posing as a client."

Jake scowled. "I saw her about an hour ago, heading toward Papermouth Cove." He looked at Riley as if noticing him for the first time. "Who're you?"

"The cowboy," Aaron answered for him, throttling up the motor. "Let's go!" he called back to his brother.

The other boat kept pace with them as they flew east,

snippets of Jake's explanation to his passenger rising over the roar of the motors and the wind. Apparently, even the client knew about Hannah and her Wyoming ordeal. Small towns were small towns, whether Wyoming or Alabama.

"We're close," Aaron told him. "Just around that bend."

Riley just prayed they'd be in time.

"SO, I WAS RIGHT." Hannah was surprised by how calm she felt, now that the moment of confrontation had arrived. Maybe it was the feel of the knife in her right hand. She whispered a silent prayer of thanks that she'd been conscientious about keeping the hinge oiled; the blade had easily and silently opened for her with just a flick of her fingers.

"I certainly gave you enough clues," the man who called himself Ken Lassiter said with a soft chuckle. He reached into the tackle box beside him and pulled out a yellow, nylon fish stringer.

Hannah eyed his hands as he started wrapping the end of the stringer around one hand. One loop. Two.

"No blitz attack?" she asked aloud. "No face full of pepper spray?"

He shook his head. "You'd be expecting that. I like to keep an element of surprise."

"Your name isn't Ken Lassiter."

"No, it's not." He smiled more broadly. "Nice clue, though, wasn't it? Ken Lassiter, Lassiter Oil—you do remember that, don't you?"

Hannah ran her finger over the flat side of the knife blade, clinging to the steady calm she'd so far managed to retain. "Is this really all about proving me wrong?"

"You didn't listen to my warning."

"I didn't realize that was a killing offense."

His smile faded. "You never think about the people whose lives you destroy with your recklessness. What about your parents, waiting at home for your return? What if you'd had a husband or children?"

"You'd have made sure I didn't get back to them, if you'd gotten your way." She felt panic and anger battling in the pit of her stomach. She tamped down both emotions. "What's your real name?"

"Kyle Layton." He answered the question as if he was swatting away a bug. His face reddened and his voice rose. "I didn't get my way. You chose your own path. You tempted fate." His voice dipped to a disgusted growl. "You all do."

It was a little harder maintaining her calm when he was starting to unravel in front of her, but she forced herself to react as if he was rational, knowing that if she could stall for time, someone would eventually wander by the cove and she'd have a better chance at a clean escape. She kept her voice steady as she asked, "You know a lot of women who've tempted fate?"

"My whole life," Layton answered, his voice softening to an almost childlike tone. "He told her not to go to Laramie. He could've made ends meet by himself. She didn't need to take a job so far away."

Somewhere behind her, Hannah heard the sound of motors nearing the opening of the cove. She'd have a narrow window of opportunity to get their attention, but she didn't dare telegraph her plans to the man coming apart in front of her.

"Are you talking about your mother?" she asked him.

He looked up, his gaze swimming into focus as if he'd forgotten she was there with him. "Yes. My mother."

"What happened to her?" she asked, trying to keep her voice sympathetic.

"She was working late at the store. That bastard she worked for had her close up alone." The little boy timbre of his voice grew more pronounced, tinged with a childlike anger and hurt. "Daddy told her not to take the job, and he was right!" Layton turned a wounded animal gaze on her. "She did this to us! She didn't listen, and she did this to us!"

Oh, my God, she realized, her blood chilling to an icy crawl. *He's been killing his mother, over and over again.*

Behind her, nearing the cove's mouth, the sound of motors grew louder. At least two, running close together. It was odd enough to distract her for a moment.

Long enough for Layton to grab the heavy, metal tackle box and swing it at her head.

She ducked at the last minute, and the tackle box grazed her temple. It hurt like hell, but she didn't see stars or lose her balance. As he started to swing again, she pulled out the knife and slashed at his arm.

He roared in pain and rage, body-slamming her in response. They both toppled from the boat into the lake.

The shock of the cold water almost made her gasp, but she was half submerged, and the last thing she needed was a lung full of water. She rose back to the surface and drew a long breath, struggling to free herself from Layton's flailing grip.

Suddenly, something pressed against her throat, pulling tight. Black spots dotted her vision as she tried to stay focused. He was using the fish stringer as a makeshift garrote. She felt the rough nylon digging into her throat.

She tightened her grip on the knife, fighting the onslaught of darkness and silence. Her entire consciousness seemed to narrow to the cold, hard feel of the knife clutched in her fist.

With the last of her strength, she jabbed hard behind her and felt the blade connect with something soft.

The grip on the fish stringer loosened, and the world rushed back in a firestorm of colors and sounds.

Water, cold as the tomb, swallowing her whole. The bubbly sound of Kyle Layton's gasps for air behind her. Boat motors, shrieking at full throttle, filling her ears with white noise before the engines idled down to a low hum.

Kyle Layton released her, and she kicked away from him, racing for the rocky shoreline thirty yards away. She didn't care who was behind her or what happened to Layton. She just wanted to get as far from him as possible.

She reached the bank and scrambled over the rocks and mud to the grassy edge beyond. Once there, she tried to stand, but the world around her went into a swirling taildive. Her knees buckled beneath her and she pitched forward into the grass. She lay still and willed her head to stop spinning long enough for her to enjoy the simple pleasure of still being alive.

AARON COOPER DROVE HIS BOAT into the mouth of Papermouth Cove just in time for Riley to witness Kyle Layton's blitz attack. He yelled in horror as the tackle box made contact with the side of Hannah's head.

Aaron poured on the speed. "Hold on!"

They were within fifty yards when Layton tackled Hannah and they both flew into the water with a booming splash.

The next thirty yards seemed to take forever to traverse. Guiding the boat closer, Aaron howled out a stream of profanity that would put even a roughneck cowboy to shame.

The struggle continued in the water, until Hannah suddenly broke free and started racing toward the shore, her swimming strokes growing increasingly sluggish and erratic as she neared the bank. In the water, Kyle Layton started paddling away from the crappie boat, his movements jerky and slow.

For a moment, Riley couldn't take his eyes off the man, all the rage and grief of three long years focusing like a laser on the man's feeble escape attempt. The urge to grab his Ruger and end the struggle was almost more than Riley could resist.

Then, out of the corner of his eye, he saw Hannah make it to shore and immediately crumple to the ground. All thought of Layton, of the sweet siren call of revenge, dissipated like smoke in the wind.

"Hannah!" A hissing stream of fears ran through his mind like a litany, threatening to drown out rational thought.

"I'll get Layton," Aaron shouted.

Riley threw off his jacket and jerked at his boots, cursing when one stuck. It finally came free. He tossed it aside and plunged into the cold lake water.

He covered the remaining distance to the shore in a few frantic strokes and pulled himself on to the bank, his heart pounding like a bass drum in his chest. Scrambling over the rocks, he reached her still, crumpled form. He felt for her carotid pulse, praying silently.

At his touch, she jerked away. Her eyes opened, wildly fighting for focus. It took a second for her to react to what she was seeing.

"Riley?" Her voice, raspy and weak, rang with surprise.

He found himself laughing at her shocked expression, so grateful she was alive that the whole world suddenly seemed like a bright, beautiful place.

She didn't resist when he grabbed her up and crushed her to him, pressing kisses over her cheeks, in her hair, and finally hard and sweet against her lips.

The fingers feebly clutching his arms tightened, their grip strengthening. Beneath his mouth, her lips moved, parting with invitation.

He threaded his fingers through her hair, holding her face steady as he poured into the kiss all his pent up fears, longings and hopes. When he finished, he drew his head back and gazed into her beautiful, liquid gaze.

"Why aren't you in Wyoming?" she asked.

"Because I love you," he answered with a laugh.

A glorious smile curved her kiss-stung lips. "I didn't think you'd ever figure that out on your own, cowboy," she drawled, running her thumb over his bottom lip.

He dragged her closer, heat flooding his belly. "Cowboys always need a sidekick, darlin'." He tangled his hand in her hair, drawing her head back to give him access to the bruised skin of her throat. Anger coiled like a rattler in his chest, but he killed it. There'd be time to sort out justice later.

Right now, he wanted Hannah to know just how damned much he loved her.

A long, thorough kiss later, they came up for air. "Just to be clear," he murmured against the curve of her ear, "you love me too, right?"

She nipped at the tendon on the side of his neck. "From the top of your Stetson to the soles of your ratty old snake-skin boots."

When he laughed, he realized that it was the first time in three years that he felt truly, unreservedly happy.

Epilogue

Five months later

"People around here call you my cowboy," Hannah murmured in Riley's ear as he led her slowly across the pavilion that had turned into a dance floor for their wedding reception.

He tucked her hand against his heart and smiled down at her from beneath the brim of his Stetson. "Why ever would they do that, darlin'?"

"Maybe it's the boots," she murmured, reaching up to tip his hat back a notch. "Or the horse trailer hitched to your truck. Or—"

He shushed her with a kiss that would have made her toes tingle even if her feet weren't stuffed into pointed white pumps. "I'm sorry Luke couldn't make it."

She tried not to let a thread of sadness taint the happiness of her wedding day. "He'll come back, sooner or later. We all do." She looked into his happy, blue eyes. "Are you sure you're okay relocating here? Won't you miss Joe and Jane?"

Riley looked over his shoulder at his friend, who sat at one of the tables flanking the dance floor. Joe was holding his newborn son in his arms, while Jane chatted happily with

Hannah's sister-in-law Mariah, who held her own little boy, Micah, on her lap. "He has his own family," Riley said with a smile. "And now I have mine. They're as close as a phone or e-mail. We won't lose touch."

She closed her eyes and relaxed into his embrace, setting aside any lingering worries. He'd miss Wyoming, even though he swore he wouldn't, but life was a series of choices with consequences. She'd make sure he never felt that trading Wyoming for Alabama was a bad bargain.

Riley cleared his throat. "There's one other thing."

She looked up, a little concerned by the frown lining his brow. "What?"

"Kyle Layton was convicted last week. They gave him life without parole."

"Oh." She hadn't thought about Layton for a couple of months. He'd pleaded guilty to assault in an Alabama court, perhaps hoping he could avoid prosecution in Wyoming, but once Joe, Riley and Sheriff Tanner had his identity confirmed, they'd been able to piece together enough physical evidence against him to bring him up on multiple murder charges in Wyoming. Alabama had waived extradition and sent him to Wyoming for trial.

"Does that mean he'll be jailed up there instead of here?"

"Yeah, that's the latest."

"Then it's really over."

He nodded, pressing his lips to her forehead. "How about we stop talking about that and start talking about what naughty, naughty things you're going to do to me when you get me alone?"

She laughed, rising up to bite his earlobe. "How about we get the hell out of here and let me show you instead?"

He looked down at her, love and hunger shining from his blue eyes. "On the count of three. One. Two. Three!"

Joining hands, they raced off the dance floor together, the whole wide world in front of them.

* * * * *

*Don't miss the next book in the
Cooper Justice miniseries when
CHICKASAW COUNTY CAPTIVE goes on sale
in February 2010, only from Paula Graves
and Harlequin Intrigue!*

"Aren't you going to say 'Fly me' or at least 'Welcome Aboard'?"

Amanda Bauer didn't. The softly muttered word that actually came out of her mouth was a lot less welcoming. And had fewer letters. Four, to be exact.

The man shook his head and tsked. "Not exactly the friendly skies. Haven't caught the spirit yet this morning?"

"Make one more airline-slogan crack and you'll be walking to Chicago," she said.

He nodded once, then pushed his sunglasses onto the top of his tousled hair. The move revealed blue eyes that matched the sky above. And yeah. They were twinkling. Damn it.

"Understood. Just, uh, promise me you'll say 'Coffee, tea or me' at least once, okay? Please?"

Amanda tried to glare, but that twinkle sucked the annoyance right out of her. She could only draw in a slow breath as he climbed into the plane. As she watched her passenger disappear into the small jet, she had to wonder about the trip she was about to take.

Coffee and tea they had, and he was welcome to them. But her? Well, she'd never even considered making a move on a customer before. Talk about unprofessional.

And yet…

Something inside her suddenly wanted to take a chance, to be a little outrageous.

How long since she had done indecent things—or decent ones, for that matter—with a sexy man? Not since before they'd thrown all their energies into expanding Clear-Blue Air, at the very least. She hadn't had time for a lunch date, much less the kind of lust-fest she'd enjoyed in her younger years. The kind that lasted for entire weekends and involved not leaving a bed except to grab the kind of sensuous food that could be smeared onto—and eaten off—someone else's hot, naked, sweat-tinged body.

She closed her eyes, her hand clenching tight on the railing. Her heart fluttered in her chest and she tried to make herself move. But she couldn't—not climbing up, but not backing away, either. Not physically, and not in her head.

Was she really considering this? God, she hadn't even looked at the stranger's left hand to make sure he was available. She had no idea if he was actually attracted to her or just an irrepressible flirt. Yet something inside was telling her to take a shot with this man.

It was crazy. Something she'd never considered. Yet right now, at this moment, she was definitely considering it. If he was available…could she do it? Seduce a stranger. Have an anonymous fling, like something out of a blue movie on late-night cable?

She didn't know. All she knew was that the flight to Chicago was a short one so she had to decide quickly. And as she put her foot on the bottom step and began to climb up, Amanda suddenly had to wonder if she was about to embark on the ride of her life.

Sold, bought, bargained for or bartered

He'll take his…

Bride on Approval

Whether there's a debt to be paid,
a will to be obeyed or a business
to be saved…she has no choice
but to say, "I do"!

PURE PRINCESS, BARTERED BRIDE
by *Caitlin Crews*
#2894

Available February 2010!

REQUEST YOUR FREE BOOKS!

2 FREE NOVELS
PLUS 2
FREE GIFTS!

✦ HARLEQUIN®

INTRIGUE®

Breathtaking Romantic Suspense

YES! Please send me 2 FREE Harlequin Intrigue® novels and my 2 FREE gifts (gifts are worth about $10). After receiving them, if I don't wish to receive any more books, I can return the shipping statement marked "cancel." If I don't cancel, I will receive 6 brand-new novels every month and be billed just $4.24 per book in the U.S. or $4.99 per book in Canada. That's a saving of close to 15% off the cover price! It's quite a bargain! Shipping and handling is just 50¢ per book in the U.S. and 75¢ per book in Canada.* I understand that accepting the 2 free books and gifts places me under no obligation to buy anything. I can always return a shipment and cancel at any time. Even if I never buy another book from Harlequin, the two free books and gifts are mine to keep forever.

182 HDN E4EC   382 HDN E4EN

Name	(PLEASE PRINT)	
Address		Apt. #
City	State/Prov.	Zip/Postal Code

Signature (if under 18, a parent or guardian must sign)

Mail to the **Harlequin Reader Service:**
IN U.S.A.: P.O. Box 1867, Buffalo, NY 14240-1867
IN CANADA: P.O. Box 609, Fort Erie, Ontario L2A 5X3
Not valid for current subscribers to Harlequin Intrigue books.

**Are you a subscriber to Harlequin Intrigue books and
want to receive the larger-print edition? Call 1-800-873-8635 today!**

* Terms and prices subject to change without notice. Prices do not include applicable taxes. N.Y. residents add applicable sales tax. Canadian residents will be charged applicable provincial taxes and GST. Offer not valid in Quebec. This offer is limited to one order per household. All orders subject to approval. Credit or debit balances in a customer's account(s) may be offset by any other outstanding balance owed by or to the customer. Please allow 4 to 6 weeks for delivery. Offer available while quantities last.

Your Privacy: Harlequin is committed to protecting your privacy. Our Privacy Policy is available online at www.eHarlequin.com or upon request from the Reader Service. From time to time we make our lists of customers available to reputable third parties who may have a product or service of interest to you. If you would prefer we not share your name and address, please check here. ☐

Help us get it right—We strive for accurate, respectful and relevant communications. To clarify or modify your communication preferences, visit us at www.ReaderService.com/consumerschoice.

HI10

HARLEQUIN
Ambassadors

Want to share your passion for reading Harlequin® Books?

Become a Harlequin Ambassador!

Harlequin Ambassadors are a group of passionate and well-connected readers who are willing to share their joy of reading Harlequin® books with family and friends.

You'll be sent all the tools you need to spark great conversation, including free books!

All we ask is that you share the romance with your friends and family!

You'll also be invited to have a say in new book ideas and exchange opinions with women just like you!

To see if you qualify* to be a Harlequin Ambassador, please visit www.HarlequinAmbassadors.com.

*Please note that not everyone who applies to be a Harlequin Ambassador will qualify. For more information please visit www.HarlequinAmbassadors.com.

Thank you for your participation.

BAP09BPA